TUCKER'S TREASURE

TUCKER'S
TREASURE

•

ROBIN GIBSON

AVALON BOOKS
THOMAS BOUREGY AND COMPANY, INC.
401 LAFAYETTE STREET
NEW YORK, NEW YORK 10003

PRINTED IN THE UNITED STATES OF AMERICA
ON ACID-FREE PAPER
BY HADDON CRAFTSMEN, SCRANTON, PENNSYLVANIA

To my brother,
Harold Lee

Chapter One

Four men sat on exhausted horses. Weariness cut hard lines in their faces as they waited on a ridge overlooking the stage road. Dust clung to the stubble on their cheeks, and wary expressions rode on their faces.

Their leader, a tall man, unhooked a canteen from his saddle and took a long drink. Without a word, he replaced the stopper and passed the canteen to his companions.

"Tucker, we gotta stop. We can't go on riding like this," Danny Wheeler complained.

"Shut up kid," Hardy growled, accepting the canteen from Weaver. From the first, Hardy had opposed taking the kid into the group.

Danny's eyes narrowed, his temper flaring, but he held his tongue. Nobody crossed Hardy, not even the boss. Danny stole a look at the boss. Tucker sat on his horse, running his fingers through his dark hair, as he stared down at the stage road.

"The kid's right, Tucker. We've got to stop. These hosses are just about done in," Weaver advised. Weaver was a big man with a shock of wild hair, already turning gray.

Tucker glanced at the horses. They stood with their heads hanging low. Weaver was right; they had to stop.

"How long till the stage is due?" Tucker asked.

Weaver drew a huge gold watch from his pocket. He stared at the watch, then looked to the sky. Holding up his

1

hand, he counted off his fingers, then rubbed his chin. "Anytime, I reckon," he replied.

"Alright, let's find some shade. We'll rest until the stage passes," Tucker decided.

Still several miles away, the stage moved slowly in the heat. Inside the stage, four occupants sat in uncomfortable seats. Three of the passengers were men, the fourth a young lady, Martha Flynn.

She leaned back in her seat and sighed. So far this trip had been a great disappointment. She had imagined the stage racing from stop to stop, where they would be greeted by a frenzy of motion as the team was exchanged for fresh horses.

Instead, the coach plodded over what passed for a road. They moved slow enough so that each of the weary passengers felt every single bump in the road.

The stops at local ranches for fresh horses did little to enhance the romantic image of the West. The horses were efficiently changed by grim-looking men who spoke little or not at all.

A determined expression set on her face, Martha dabbed at the perspiration streaming down her face with a lace handkerchief. So things were different than she had imagined; big deal, this wasn't a sight-seeing trip. Still, if the stage went faster a breeze might come through the window.

Martha's mind wandered to a cool meadow, high in the mountains. In her mind she could see a lake of deep clear water. The vision became so clear that she could almost feel the breeze across the water.

But then the stage hit a deep rut in the road, throwing Martha against the side of the coach, and the spell was broken.

Swabbing her neck with the damp handkerchief, Marty

studied the man seated just across from her. For the whole trip, all he had done was sleep. Whenever the stage stopped, he would get out and stretch his legs, but never made any attempt to talk with his fellow passengers.

Marty killed time fantasizing about him. In her mind he was an old gunfighter, riding the stage home to meet a child he never knew.

Taking another look at the man, Marty almost laughed at herself. He sure didn't look like a gunfighter. He looked more like an old prospector. Maybe he was. Maybe he had struck it rich and was going to file his claim!

One of the other passengers, a rough-looking man with a hardset jaw, pulled a canteen from underneath his seat. He started to take a drink, then stopped. "Would you like a drink, Miss Flynn?" he asked, holding the canteen out.

"Why thank you, Mister Benedict," she replied, flashing a smile at Benedict, "but please call me Marty. Miss Flynn sounds so formal."

"May we inquire as to what brings such a lovely young lady out to this part of the country?" asked a portly gentleman in a rumpled suit.

Marty laughed, her bright laughter filling the tiny coach. "Why certainly, Mister Talbot," she replied cheerfully. "I came looking for a man named Tucker."

Talbot and Benedict exchanged worried glances. Marty wanted to laugh at them. Their reaction to Tucker's name was exactly what she expected. Benedict started to speak, while Talbot stroked his beard.

What caught Marty's attention was the old man across from her. The mention of Tucker's name brought his eyes wide open. All of a sudden, Marty got the eerie feeling that he hadn't been sleeping at all.

He didn't say anything, he just eyed Marty curiously. Marty noticed his eyes were clear and bright blue, with a hint of laughter in them. The laughter didn't spread to the rest of his face, though. His jaw remained set firm, like smiling was a luxury he didn't allow himself.

Talbot cleared his throat noisily, looking to Benedict for support. "Miss Flynn, I don't think Tucker is a good man for a lady such as yourself to be associating with," he said finally.

"He's right," Benedict agreed. "I've met Tucker, and he's a wild and rowdy man. Why, he's wanted in two states."

Marty laughed again. "Believe me, gentlemen, I have no intention of associating with Tucker. I merely wish to hire him for a job," Marty assured them.

"Miss Flynn, I must urge you to take caution. I have never met the infamous Tucker, but his reputation precedes him," Talbot said. A look of doubt replaced the concern on his face. "What kind of problem could you possibly have that would require the services of a man like Tucker?"

The laughter drained from Marty's face, replaced quickly by sadness. A tear rolled down her cheeks; she dabbed at it daintily with her hanky. "It's my brother," she answered in a choked voice. "He's been taken captive by Apaches. I want Tucker to go rescue him."

Benedict grunted and swore softly. "I don't want to upset you, Miss Flynn, but your brother is more than likely dead."

"I'm afraid he's probably right," Talbot agreed solemnly. "Besides, even if your brother were alive still, I doubt if even Tucker could go fetch him."

Marty gave them each a brave smile. "You may well be right, but I wouldn't feel right if I didn't try everything, and Tucker is my last hope."

Talbot and Benedict both shook their heads. Evidently, Marty had no idea what going into Apache country meant. Benedict cleared his throat and tried to explain. "Miss

Flynn, you must understand, this is quite an undertaking. Mostly, when a body goes into Indian country, he tries to sneak through real quiet like. You go hunting for Apaches and you'll find them alright—a plenty of them!''

"That's right, Miss Flynn. Tucker may be crazy, but he ain't stupid. Nobody in their right mind would attempt such a rescue."

"I'm prepared to offer a substantial sum of money," Marty said, looking at the two men hopefully.

"Now, that ain't a good idea at all," Benedict told her. "Tucker would likely just take your money and ride away."

"If Tucker says he'll do the job and takes your money, he'll either find your brother or die trying," the old man across from Marty put in quietly.

Talbot coughed into his hand and looked out the window, making it very clear that he disagreed with the old man.

"So you think Tucker can be trusted?" Marty asked, anxious to hear the old man's opinion.

"Yes ma'am. If he gives you his word, you can take it as gospel," he replied, ignoring Talbot and Benedict.

"Are you a friend of Tucker's?" Talbot asked, looking pointedly at the old man.

For the first time, the old man smiled. "A friend of Tucker's?" He shook his head slowly. "No, I wouldn't say that. Fact is, I've been looking for Tucker myself. I'm gonna kill him!''

Benedict snorted, and asked sarcastically, "And just who might you be?"

"I'm Deke Carlin," the old man replied quietly.

The name meant nothing to Marty, but it sure meant something to both Talbot and Benedict. Smiling, she watched the wind leave their sails. Benedict's face flamed red, and Talbot seemed to have something stuck in his throat. Marty's amusement faded as she realized just what Carlin had said.

Marty stamped her foot on the floor of the stage, giving Carlin a severe look. "That won't do, Mister Carlin. I told you I need Tucker to find my brother. I want you to give me your word you won't kill him till he finds my brother."

A slow, red flush began to creep up Deke Carlin's face, but he held Marty's eye steadily with his own intense gaze. "Alright ma'am, I'll wait, but as soon as he comes back with your brother, I'm gonna kill him for sure."

"That's your own business, Mister Carlin, but I'll have you know that I do not approve," Marty replied sharply, as the stage hit another rut in the road.

Tucker and his men lay in a small nest of rocks above the trail. Of the four, only Tucker remained awake, his eyes busily scanning the terrain with the watchfulness of a hunter or the hunted.

To the casual eye, Tucker might not appear wary, for he slouched against a boulder, his rifle draped casually across his knees. An unlit cigarette dangled loosely from the corner of his mouth.

To any casual observer, Tucker seemed to be completely at ease with his surroundings, even a trifle bored. Which was just what Tucker wanted the world to think.

Tucker had made his brag that anything anybody could do, he could do better. "Including drinking, cussin', fighting, and loving," he would always add solemnly.

To date, Tucker had made his brag stand up. And there had been challenges, dozens of them. But so far none had bested Tucker.

For a man who put on an outward appearance of bravado,

Tucker possessed a healthy streak of caution. A streak which became wider with each passing year.

At twenty-six, Tucker found times when he yearned for a quieter life. He still loved the thrills, but all of the running and hiding took their toll.

Tucker yawned and rubbed his tired eyes. Shifting positions, Tucker reached for his canteen. Immediately, Tucker heard a metallic click, and saw a slight movement from one of the sleeping men.

"It's okay, Hardy, I'm just getting a drink," Tucker said softly.

Pulling the cork from the canteen, Tucker smiled, but with no humor. Tucker knew that if he'd reached for the saddlebags instead of the canteen, he would be dead now.

But that was Hardy. He never trusted anyone or any situation, which was why the half-Indian survived so many years in such a dangerous business.

Tucker raised the canteen to his lips and rinsed his mouth. Spitting the water on a rock, Tucker considered his companions. Of them all, only Weaver could be called a friend. The kid maybe, but Tucker wasn't sure about him. The kid was too hot tempered for Tucker's tastes. Likely get them all killed someday. Shaking his head sadly, Tucker wished the stage would hurry.

Maybe they shouldn't have waited on the stage. No, being out in the open on tired horses was a good way to get caught. Soon as the stage came by, they could move out, mixing their tracks in with the ones on the road.

Frowning, Tucker reviewed their getaway to see what went wrong. Somewhere, they had fallen behind schedule. They had left the bank in good time. Tucker would bet it was at least ten minutes before the posse got organized to pursue them.

They'd ran their horses for an hour to a spot where

Tucker had spares waiting. Leaving their worn out horses for the posse to find, they pushed on. Not running, but still hustling. The rest of the afternoon they rode, and on into the night.

Around midnight, they came to the deserted homestead where Tucker left the other set of fresh horses. From there they rode slower. Sure of their lead on the posse, the gang started making their tracks harder to find.

On the stage road was where Tucker planned to lose the posse for good. They would turn west following the stage road, turning south one at a time.

Tucker had already ridden over the trail once and selected the spots they would leave the trail. Hardy would turn south first. He would leave the trail on the crest of a caprock ridge, where his tracks would be hard to spot. Weaver would go south along a sandy draw. The loose sand wouldn't hold his tracks for very long. Hardy would follow a trail used by the migrant sheepherders.

As for himself, Tucker wasn't quite sure where he would turn south—or even if he would. He carried the saddlebags with the money, he could keep going west. Out to California maybe?

Tucker glanced at the sleeping men, wondering what they would do if he left with the money. Weaver might chalk it up to experience and forget it. Who knew what the kid would do, but the kid didn't worry Tucker. Hardy now, he was a different story. He wouldn't forget, not in this lifetime anyway. He would hunt Tucker till his dying day, and that bothered Tucker.

The sound of the stage cut through Tucker's thoughts. Looking back down the trail, Tucker spotted the stage, still well over a mile away. Taking off his hat, Tucker ran a grimy sleeve across his forehead.

"Something's follerin' the stage," Hardy commented quietly.

Tucker glanced at Hardy curiously. Sometimes he wondered if the man ever slept. "Is it the posse?"

Hardy shrugged. "It could be. Whoever it is, they're moving fast."

"Wake the others and get the horses ready," Tucker ordered, struggling to see what Hardy saw. Then he spotted it, a dust cloud behind and to the south of the stage.

Taking a last look at the stage, Tucker turned and went to help the others saddle the horses. "Group of riders following the stage. They might be the posse, so let's keep it quiet," Tucker ordered, throwing his saddle on his bay.

After tightening his cinch, Tucker slid his rifle down in the boot on the saddle. Under Hardy's ever watchful eye, Tucker tossed the saddlebags across his horse's neck.

Giving Hardy a big grin, Tucker gathered his reins and led the bay over to the edge of the rocks.

The men chasing the stage had caught it. They had stopped almost directly beneath Tucker and his men.

"Shoot, they're holding up the stage," Weaver said, in disgust. "Why would they be doing a dang fool thing like that? Everybody knows there ain't never no money on stages."

Tucker swore, feeling the same disgust as Weaver, but for a different reason. Now, there would be another posse combing the country, making their own escape more difficult.

The five bandits grouped around the stage. The holdup looked to be going smoothly, the outlaws pointing their guns at the driver. Waving his pistol at the top of the coach, the outlaw leader said something to the stage driver. The driver shook his head, spreading his hands in front of him. Tucker was wishing they would hurry up, when a man rolled out of the stage, his gun belching fire.

"That's Deke Carlin!" Tucker cried, leaping on the bay.

The bay leapt forward, responding instantly to the spurs. Tucker pulled his gun as they plunged recklessly down the rocky slope.

Tucker could see that two of the bandits were already down as he reached the bottom of the slope. Tucker snapped a shot at the outlaw nearest him and missed. The man spun around, his eyes wide with surprise.

Before Tucker could fire again, a rifle shot sounded from up the slope. Tucker could hear the bullet strike, as it knocked the outlaw over backward.

Jerking the bay around, Tucker spurred him around to the other side of the stage. Deke Carlin sat on the ground, blood flowing from his left arm. Despite the wound, Carlin tried to plug fresh shells in his gun.

One of the bandits had dropped his gun and was drawing his rifle. The other was trying to swing his horse around for a shot at Carlin.

Without thinking, Tucker shot the man drawing the rifle. Swinging his horse around, Tucker saw the last bandit shoot at Deke Carlin. The bullet hit the wheel of the stage, sending a shower of splinters flying.

Turning and firing across his body, Tucker fired three times, as fast as he could cock and pull the trigger. The bullets swept the man off his horse like a giant, invisible hand.

In the silence which followed the battle, Tucker began to reload his pistol. The gun fully loaded now, Tucker dismounted, leaving the reins trailing in the dirt.

"Turn around, Tucker!"

Tucker felt a chill from the deadly seriousness of the

order. Tucker turned to see Deke Carlin standing, his back braced against the stagecoach. Deke's left arm hung limply at his side. Big drops of blood dripped from his fingertips, but the pistol in his right hand was rock steady, as he held it trained right on Tucker's stomach.

Chapter Two

"I just wanted you to know I was the one who killed you," Deke Carlin said in a flat tone.

Tucker looked into the slate-gray eyes for any chances at all. The eyes could have been chipped out of granite for all the feeling they showed.

"My men are up on the ridge. If you was to kill me, they'd finish you off," Tucker replied, wondering if he could get off a shot in time. He held his pistol, but it pointed straight down. Slower to raise and fire than draw, but Tucker knew he'd have to chance it.

"Mister Carlin! I am ashamed of you," a feminine voice called shrilly, from inside the stage. "You promised not to kill him," Marty called, jumping out of the coach.

Deke Carlin bowed his head like a schoolboy before the headmaster. "You're right, ma'am. In the excitement, I plumb forgot," he mumbled.

Amazed at the change in the man's attitude, Tucker snickered under his breath. Instantly, Carlin's head snapped up, his cold eyes boring twin holes into Tucker. "You wipe that smile off your face, or I swear I'll forget my promise to the lady and kill you right here," Carlin threatened.

With some effort Tucker managed to put on a more serious expression. "Anything you say, Deke."

As a group, Tucker's men rode up to the stage. Each man knew about Deke Carlin's vow to kill Tucker. They watched the old man with guarded eyes.

Weaver nodded his head in Deke's direction. "How are you, Deke?" he asked.

"I'm shot, that's how I am," Deke replied testily. "I see you're still riding in bad company."

Weaver grinned ruefully. "Aw, Deke, you hadn't ought to say such things. They're good boys."

Carlin snorted and started to reply, but Hardy beat him. "A passel of folks coming up the trail," the dark outlaw said.

Tucker squinted his eyes, staring into the bright mirage. He could barely make out the approaching riders. They looked unnaturally tall in the distance. As they approached, Tucker saw the star pinned to the chest of the leader.

Deke Carlin saw the star as well. "You boys are on your own," he said, sliding his gun into the holster.

The riders began to fan out as they came closer. About twenty feet away, the leader stopped. "Tucker, you and your men are under arrest for robbing the bank in Silver City," he called out.

Tucker threw back his head and laughed. "Why, Sheriff, you got it all wrong. We just came along and stopped this here stage holdup."

"Then you won't mind if I look through your saddlebags," the sheriff said.

"I wouldn't advise it," Tucker replied quietly.

"Before you gentlemen shoot yourselves to pieces, could I have a word with Mister Tucker?" Marty Flynn asked.

"Now hold on a minute, Miss. This man just robbed our bank. It's my sworn duty to take him in," the sheriff protested.

"*Allegedly* robbed the bank," Marty flung back. "You have no proof they robbed anything. Besides, I only need a couple of minutes."

The sheriff twisted his pale mustache between his fingers.

"Alright, lady, you got one minute," he decided. He stood in the stirrups, stabbing at Tucker with his finger. "Don't you go getting any ideas. Bob's going to have a rifle trained on you the whole time. Any sudden move will be your last!"

To punctuate the order, one of the deputies leveled his rifle at Tucker's forehead. Both amused and confused, Tucker glanced from the rifle to Marty, then over to his men. Weaver met Tucker's eyes, and shrugged his heavy shoulders.

"Mister Tucker, if you would join me," Marty requested, beckoning for Tucker to follow her away from the others.

Her tone made it sound a lot like an order, and he felt tempted to refuse. But curiosity got the better of him. Dropping the reins, he followed her. He was admiring the swing of her hips, when she spun to confront him. "I have a proposition for you, Mister Tucker," she said.

"First of all, lady, it ain't Mister Tucker. My name is Tucker Evans."

"Sorry. Tucker is all I ever heard you called. My name is Marty Flynn. As I said, I have a proposition for you."

"Lady, in case you ain't taken notice, I'm just a little bit busy right at the moment."

"Oh, you mean that sheriff?" Marty asked, waving her hand in the direction of the posse. "They won't bother us."

Tucker shook his head, rolling his eyes. "I suppose you are just going to shoo them away?"

"Something like that," Marty said. "Now, about my proposition?"

Tucker started to leave, but then changed his mind. "What kind of a deal did you have in mind?"

"My brother has been taken captive by Indians. I want you and your men to go rescue him."

"Lady, you are crazy. Why would I want to get myself killed?" Tucker said, laughing out loud.

Marty laughed, giving Tucker an amused look. "Why, Mister Evans, I thought there wasn't anything you wouldn't try at least once," Marty replied, enjoying the tightening around Tucker's eyes. "Besides, I'm willing to pay ten thousand dollars."

"Now, that does make a difference," Tucker conceded cautiously. "Fifteen grand might make all the difference," he added slyly.

"Oh, I think you will agree to ten thousand," Marty said, smiling confidently.

Tucker backed up a step. Being a gambler, he judged people pretty well. Instinct warned him that she had an ace up her sleeve. "You are pretty sure of yourself," he observed. "What makes you think I won't tell you to take a hike?"

"Oh, I don't think you will," Marty said sweetly. "Your saddlebags look awfully full to me. If I were to guess, I'd say the sheriff is right."

"That's no more your business than it is his. What I keep in my saddlebags is my own concern," Tucker countered, then smiled confidently. "Anyway, I don't think the sheriff is willing to die just to find out."

"You're right about that, I think," Marty agreed, looking past Tucker to the posse. "They do seem a bit nervous."

Tucker showed her a crooked grin. "They're a bit antsy alright. I don't think they will make an issue of it," he predicted.

"You are probably right," Marty said, patting Tucker's arm and giving him a dazzling smile. "Of course, if I were to tell them I saw the money in your bag."

"You wouldn't dare," Tucker replied easily.

"Oh, don't be too sure. I'd do anything to help my brother," Marty warned.

"Lady, don't cross me. Maybe you don't know who you're dealing with. If you did you wouldn't dare push me."

Marty threw back her head and laughed. Mischief dancing in her eyes, she stepped around Tucker and waved to the sheriff. "Sheriff . . . sheriff," she called, waving her arm in the air.

"Aw, crud hell," Tucker groaned, throwing his hat down and kicking it across the ground. When Marty opened her mouth to holler at the sheriff, Tucker grabbed her arm. "I'm warning you lady, don't mess with me!"

Tucker groaned as Marty shot him a sparkling smile, then yelled to the sheriff. "I don't think you will need to search Mister Evans' saddlebags. I saw the money in them."

Swearing bitterly, Tucker stomped his hat. Still holding Marty by the arm, he jerked her close. "Lady, you are about to make me mad," he said, grinding his teeth.

"I'm sure you will get over it," Marty replied, with a bright smile. "Now, are you going to take my offer?"

"Sure, I'll see you out in front of Yuma prison in about two years," Tucker grunted.

"Don't be silly. Yuma is in Arizona. They wouldn't send you there," Marty told him. "If you give me your word that you'll help me, I'll keep you out of jail."

"I'd like to see that," Tucker mumbled.

"Do you give me your word?" Marty persisted.

"Okay. If you can get rid of the posse, I'll go fetch your brother," Tucker agreed, never even dreaming that she could pull it off.

"I knew you would come around," Marty said, walking back to the stage. "Sheriff, I think I gave you the wrong idea," she shouted.

"How's that?" the sheriff asked, watching Tucker warily.

"When I said I saw the money in those saddlebags, I didn't mean to imply they belonged to Mister Evans or that he and his friends robbed your bank. Mister Evans took the bags off of that man's horse," she explained, pointing to the man Deke Carlin shot.

"Is that right?" the sheriff demanded harshly, his eyes boring into Tucker.

"Would you call the lady a liar?" Tucker shot back, trying hard not to laugh. Clearly the sheriff didn't want to do that, but he didn't buy the whole story either.

"Sheriff, if we get the money back, let's just drop it. We'd be a month of Sundays straightening this whole mess out," a posse member urged.

The sheriff stared at Tucker, his jaw jutting outward. Slumping in the saddle, he visibly relaxed. "Alright. Bob, go get the money. I'm not sure I believe any of this, but I ain't gonna push it." The sheriff jabbed a bony finger at Tucker. "I don't ever want to see you in my town."

Tucker didn't care for the order, nor the tone the sheriff used issuing it, but let it go.

Tucker watched with a sad expression as the deputy took the saddlebags from the bay. Tucker wasn't happy about losing all that money; he blamed Marty for that. Dang meddlesome woman!

Bob opened the bags and looked inside, a grin spreading across his face. "The money's here," he announced. "You want your bags back?" he asked, looking to Tucker.

Tucker grinned at the deputy. "They ain't mine. Like the lady said, they belong to that feller there," Tucker replied, pointing to the dead bandit. "Since they claim you can't take it with you, I don't reckon he'll miss them."

The deputy gave Tucker a mean, greasy look, but handed

the money to the sheriff without comment. The sheriff slung them across his horse's neck, much as Tucker had done earlier. "Okay men, we've got a long ways back, we'd best get started," the sheriff said, wheeling his horse around.

As they left, Weaver blew out a big sigh, wiping his forehead. "Lordy, that was close. I thought we was gonna have to ventilate a couple of them,'fore they would leave." Weaver smiled at Marty. "I gotta hand it to you, Missy, that was slicker'n calf slobbers, the way you got them to leave."

"They took our money," Hardy pointed out.

All the good humor drained from Weaver's florid face as he swore under his breath. "What you gonna do about that?" he demanded, glaring balefully at Tucker. Tucker ignored the big man, and turned to his horse.

"I suppose we best bury these fellers," the stage driver said, climbing down from the stage. "One of you got a shovel?"

Tucker laughed and winked. "I ain't got anything. Them folks took my saddlebags."

The driver gave Tucker a long hard look, then busted out laughing. "Well, I guess we'll have to use our knives."

Benedict and Talbot stumbled out of the stage, looking a little pale around the gills. "Do you mean to say that you did rob that bank?" Talbot demanded.

"Well, we went in, I poked my gun in the teller's ear and told him to give me all the money. I guess you could say we robbed the joint alright," Tucker replied, helping Weaver carry one of the dead outlaws over to where the others were scooping out a shallow grave.

"We should turn you in, when we get to town," Benedict said slowly, looking to Talbot for support.

"That's right," Talbot agreed firmly. "Don't you think we're right, Carlin?"

Deke Carlin chuckled dryly. "Being right has got a lot of folks killed," he replied, holding his wounded arm out while Marty wrapped a bandage around it.

Talbot sniffed and looked ready to argue, but something in Carlin's ice gray eyes brought him up short. With wrathful looks at Tucker, Talbot and Benedict walked around the stage and seated themselves in the shade.

Tucker ignored them as he helped dig the graves. Men like that didn't bother Tucker, but they worried the kid. "You gonna let them talk to you like that?" the kid asked loudly.

Hardy stopped digging to stare at the kid. Contempt shone in Hardy's dark eyes. Growling, Hardy spat and returned to work.

Weaver straightened, massaged his back and tried to explain it to the kid. "What are you going to do, Danny? Walk over there and shoot them?"

From his expression, it was clear that was exactly what the kid had in mind. He wanted to interrupt, but Weaver silenced the youngster with the wave of one meaty hand. "Be quiet boy, this is a time for listening."

Taking up his knife, Weaver returned to work. After a minute he stopped to look seriously at Danny. "I'll grant you that the world would probably be better off if them two was looking at grass from the bottom side, but sure as you up and killed them somebody would get worked up over it. Mostly, folks forgive and forget stealing, but kill one of their friends and they get real worked up and they stay that way. Ain't that right, Tucker?"

Tucker stopped digging to look at the stage, where Deke Carlin was still enduring Marty's care. "That's right, kid. Anyway, the sheriff in Santa Fe ain't going to care that we robbed a bank in Colorado."

Still unconvinced, Danny scowled in the direction of the

two offenders. "Least they could do was help us," he muttered.

"I reckon that's deep enough. It's too blamed hot for this kind of work," the stage driver decided. "Besides, I got a schedule to keep."

Weaver laughed, a deep, booming laugh. "You ever make it on time?"

The driver scratched the scraggly growth on his chin. "You know, I think I did come close a couple of times. Once, I couldn't have been more'n half a day late."

After the burying was completed, the old driver said a few words over the fallen men. "Well, let's get on the road," he said, clapping his hat back on his head.

As a group they walked back to the stage, where Deke Carlin stopped Tucker. "First off, I want to thank you. Reckon you saved my bacon, but I still don't figure that sets things straight. If I hadn't given my word to Miss Flynn, I'd have killed you back there."

"Sorry you feel that way, Deke," Tucker replied seriously.

"Just letting you know, you ain't off the hook for what you done. I'm warning you that you better treat that young lady right. None of your usual funny business."

Tucker laughed and gave Deke a mock salute. "Yes, sir," he replied, turning away.

"Crazy durned fool," Deke muttered, under his breath.

The stage driver was digging the shotgun out from under his seat, when Tucker reined the bay alongside the stage. "I believe I'll keep this thing a little more handy," he said wryly. "You boys 'bout had things wrapped up 'fore I got her out."

"You got it out in time to suit me," Tucker acknowledged. "Don't you have someone to ride shotgun?"

"Used to, but we ain't had no trouble for a spell, and the company begin to begrudge the money."

"Ain't that always the way?" Tucker sympathized. "Can you give me a minute to speak with the lady?"

"I suppose, but make it snappy. The grim twins are already faunching at the bit," the driver replied, waving at Benedict and Talbot.

Tucker called Marty off to the side. "Me and the boys will head south from here. We'll need half of the money now to help cover the expenses."

"South? You should be going north. My brother was captured up in Colorado."

"I thought you said he was taken by Apaches. Ain't no Apaches in Colorado," Tucker protested.

"That's what the telegraph said, that he was captured by Indians," Marty said, stubbornly.

Tucker kicked the ground in disgust. "There's other Indians besides Apaches," he informed her. "Where at in Colorado? Not Silver City, I hope."

"No. He was near the town of Del Norte. I'll go that far with you."

"Oh no you won't!" Tucker exploded. "This isn't going to be no Sunday ride in the park. This is rough country we're heading into."

"Good," Marty replied, cheerfully. "Then the scenery will be nice," she added.

Marty smiled as she watched Tucker walk away, kicking a rock and cursing under his breath. Marty couldn't help but feel smug. Tucker bought her story, hook, line and sinker. Pleased, she hurried to get her bag off the stage, while Tucker caught up one of the dead outlaws' horses for her to ride.

As they rode away, they didn't see the three posse members break away from the group. The three men pulled up on a ridge, watching the five riders.

As soon as Tucker's party disappeared from sight, the three ex-posse members followed. They were careful to keep well back and out of sight.

When the stage took off again, Deke rode outside beside the driver. He offered no explanation for the switch, so the driver figured Deke wanted some air.

"I thought you was going to kill Tucker," the driver commented.

"I will someday," Deke replied, his voice betraying no emotion. "I promised Miss Flynn I wouldn't kill Tucker until he helped her get her brother back."

"I sure did like her," the stage driver said. "I hope Tucker and his men can help her. That's a big job even for Tucker."

Deke Carlin sat quietly, stewing over the driver's words. It was a big job. "You got any objections to me taking one of those horses?"

The driver shrugged. "Don't reckon so. You figure on going to help Tucker?"

"I'm going after him anyway," Deke said, waiting for the driver to stop the stage. Talbot and Benedict poked their heads out, demanding to know what the delay was about.

Deke ignored them, and didn't bother to return the driver's wave. He had more important things to do.

Chapter Three

T ucker sat in the saddle and fumed. He didn't care for the way this whole deal was taking shape. For starters, he and Weaver were wanted in Colorado, but the main thing was having Marty along. For the fifth time he glanced back at her.

"Mister Evans, do you intend on glowering at me like an irate schoolmaster, all the way to Colorado?" Marty asked.

Grunting for an answer, Tucker turned his attention ahead. Something about Marty rubbed him the wrong way. Rubbing his jaw, Tucker tried to figure out just how he had gotten into this mess. Even now, looking back on it, Tucker couldn't quite figure out how she'd manipulated him into this. To say nothing of the fact that she'd given the bank money back.

Tucker mumbled under his breath, feeling a frustration he couldn't quite identify. "Anything wrong, boss?" Weaver asked, riding up beside Tucker.

Tucker snapped out of his muttering, glancing at the big outlaw. "Aw, nothing really. I don't like having her along," Tucker replied, turning to scowl at Marty, who stuck out her tongue.

"The kid's pretty hot under the collar about giving the money back," Weaver commented. "He claims you're losing your touch."

Tucker grinned and pushed back his hat. "I can handle

Danny,'' he allowed, then the smile drained from his face. ''What does Hardy think?''

''Who ever knows what he thinks?'' Weaver asked with a shrug. ''He don't never say nothing. I don't reckon he's too bent out of shape at you, I mean, he hasn't shot you in the back yet.''

''You've got a point there,'' Tucker said laughing. ''But if we can pull this deal off we can make twice as much as the bank job.''

''What kind of job is this?'' Weaver asked.

''Kind of a recovery job,'' Tucker replied ruefully.

''You mean like a lost gold train or something?'' Weaver asked eagerly.

''Sort of. We are going to pick up something that's been lost,'' Tucker answered vaguely.

Weaver reached across the saddle, grabbing Tucker by the arm. ''Don't feed me that batch of stinkweed,'' Weaver said, almost jerking Tucker out of the saddle. ''Just what the devil have you gotten us into this time?''

''Marty's brother has been captured by Indians. I figured we'd go fetch him,'' Tucker explained.

Weaver groaned, slapping his face with a meaty hand. ''You been wearing your hat too tight or something? You make it sound like we can just ride up and knock on the first tepee we see and they'll just hand him over.''

''I never said it would be easy, but I promised the lady,'' Tucker replied.

Weaver's face turned beet red, and he pounded his fist against his thigh. ''Tucker, I swear you gotten us mixed up in some crazy deals, but this takes the cake.''

''She's paying ten thousand dollars,'' Tucker said hastily.

Weaver dropped Tucker's arm and rubbed his jaw. ''I don't know, it still sounds crazy to me. You should have talked it over with the rest of us.'' Weaver shook his head, mulling it over. ''Ten thousand smackers, did you say?''

Tucker gave Weaver a big grin. ''Yeah, ten thousand. That'd keep us going for a while.''

Weaver licked his finger and commenced to drawing circles in the air. ''That'd be, how much apiece? Let's see . . . carry the four, add two.'' Still muttering, Weaver looked down at his hand, counting off his fingers.

''Two thousand apiece,'' Tucker supplied, grinning.

''Yeah,'' Weaver said, his voice reverent.

''That sounds pretty good, doesn't it? That much money is worth taking a few risks for, wouldn't you say?''

Weaver only grunted. The big outlaw liked the sound of ten grand, but the thought of what he had to do to get the money left him cold inside. ''I dunno, Tucker. We'd best talk it over with the others.''

''Alright, we'll talk it over when we camp tonight,'' Tucker conceded. ''Tell Hardy to drop back, and make sure we aren't being followed. I don't trust that posse.''

Weaver nodded and pulled his horse aside to let Marty and Danny pass. ''Tucker wants you to take a gander down our back-trail,'' he told Hardy. ''He thinks that sheriff mighta went and got hisself some fancy notions.''

''Tucker is right, I think,'' Hardy said, pulling a plug of tobacco from his shirt pocket. He brushed off a few grains of sand, and bit off a chew. ''What crazy thing has he got us into this time?''

Weaver shook his head. ''You ain't gonna believe it, shoot, I ain't sure I believe it. We're going to rescue the lady's brother from Indians,'' Weaver replied.

They rode a few yards in silence, Weaver watching Marty laugh at something Danny said. ''You know, I think the boss has met his match in that young filly, and he don't even know it yet. But what the heck, I like her,'' Weaver observed.

Hardy grunted and spun his horse around. "I like her too," he said softly, his voice lost in the whisper of the wind through the pines.

Tucker led them to a campsite he knew of. Snuggled down in the bottom of a tiny valley, the place was almost breathtaking. Saw-toothed ridges rose on three sides of the valley. Trees hung precariously to the steep sides of the ridges.

When they stopped, Marty almost fell from the saddle. For a second, she leaned against her horse trying to get her land legs back. Marty wasn't used to doing this much riding. While Danny and Tucker unsaddled the horses, Weaver set about making a fire.

"Hardy should be catching up to us anytime," he worried, as he coaxed a fire to life.

"You worry like an old mother hen," Tucker accused, putting together their meager pile of supplies. "Hardy can take care of himself."

"You got that right!" Danny declared. "Hardy's about the meanest critter I ever met. Now quit gabbing and start pitching that grub together. I'm 'bout starved plumb to death."

Weaver smiled across the fire at Marty as she massaged her legs. "Kids," he said disgustedly. "They're always thinking of their bellies."

Weaver slid some meat onto sticks, and propped them over the fire. When all the meat was cooking, the big outlaw wiped his hands on his jeans and shot Tucker a long meaningful look.

Ignoring Weaver, Tucker went to sit on his saddle. Pursing his lips and rubbing his jaw, Tucker considered his words carefully.

"Why don't you tell us a little more about how your brother was captured," he started. "If we are going to go get him, we'll need to know everything."

Color rushed to Marty's face, and she shot up off the ground like she'd been sitting on a cannon. "If!" she screamed. "What do you mean if? You gave me your word, Tucker Evans."

"Well, the boys thought we best talk things over a bit before we dive right in," Tucker said lamely. Feeling foolish all of a sudden, Tucker fired a dirty look at Weaver, who became very busy with his cooking in a hurry. "It didn't seem right to risk their lives without asking them first."

Danny's head jerked up and he started to speak, but Weaver cuffed him upside the head. "If you know what's good for you, you'll stay out of this one," Weaver hissed.

Calmer now, Marty returned to her seat. "I'm sorry," she said, allowing a tear to run down her cheek. "You are right, of course. If you brave men are going to risk your lives for me, I at least owe you an explanation."

Marty stopped as Hardy appeared at the edge of the firelight. Hardy gave Marty one of his rare smiles, then went to the fire. Squatting on his heels, Hardy extended his hands to the fire, watching Marty like he expected her to shoot him.

"Anybody following us?" Tucker asked.

Hardy shook his head. He reached for the pot, poured himself a cup of coffee. Sipping the coffee, he rocked back on his heels, his dark face revealing nothing.

"My brother and a party of men went into the mountains. The last letter I received from him came from Denver. I don't know if they made any other stops."

"What was their destination?" Tucker asked.

Marty hesitated. "A place called Black Canyon," she said at last. "Have you ever heard of it?"

"Yeah, I've heard of it. That's rough country. It's gonna be hard to find your brother there," Tucker replied.

"I've never heard of the place," Danny said, sneaking a hand toward the roasting meat. "What's so special about it?" Danny asked, then howled, as Weaver slapped the back of his hand.

"Keep your mitts off!" Weaver scolded. "Where did you learn your manners?" he asked, extending a piece of meat to Marty.

Sulking, Danny waited for Weaver to fish another piece of meat from the fire. "Well, what do you guys think? Are we going to help Marty?" Tucker asked, snatching the meat almost from under Danny's nose.

Danny scowled and grabbed his own food from the fire, burning his hand in the process. "How much does the job pay?" he asked, blowing on his smarting hand.

Weaver clapped the youngster on the side of the head. "The money ain't what's important. The important thing is that we'd be helping the young lady find her brother," Weaver said seriously.

"Ten thousand dollars is what I told Mister Evans," Marty said to them, holding her breath as she waited on their reply. So much depended on what they decided tonight. "That would figure out to two thousand five hundred for each of you," she added, hoping to coax them into going along.

Weaver's head shot up so fast that it almost came off it's hinges. "What?" he screamed, howling like a bloodhound with a sore paw. "You said two thousand," he accused, shaking a roasting stick in Tucker's face.

"I musta misfigured," Tucker explained easily, and

snatched a piece of meat from the stick that Weaver still brandished.

"Misfigured my butt," Weaver growled. "Why, I oughta plug you one, just on general principle."

"I will go," Hardy said, cutting into Weaver's rantings.

Weaver scowled at Hardy, as the dark outlaw rose to his feet. Hardy gave Marty a long look, then tossed the last of his coffee into the fire. As the coffee hissed and sputtered in the flames, Hardy went to his saddle and untied his bedroll. The rest of the group didn't see the sinister grin of satisfaction on his face as he moved back into the trees.

Tucker looked to the rest of his men, waiting expectantly. Weaver ran his hand over his jaw and studied the toes of his boots. Danny ate in silence, content to follow Weaver's lead.

"Alright, Tucker, I'll go, but I ain't gonna like it if you get us all killed," Weaver replied, while Danny nodded eagerly.

Chapter Four

Deke Carlin hunched over his tiny fire, the warmth of the blaze warming his tired bones. Nursing a cup of coffee, Deke tried to justify why he was here. He told himself that he merely wanted to look out for Marty Flynn.

Despite himself, Deke smiled. He liked Marty. She'd certainly set them two old windbags, Talbot and Benedict, on their cans.

The girl could use some caution, though. Especially when it came to dealing with a man like Tucker. Deke knew Tucker well, good enough to know that the crazy devil could get into more trouble before breakfast than most people could ever get out of.

Deke worried about Marty's welfare. Course, if anyone could go into Indian country and rescue a captive, it would be Tucker. The man was luckier than an outhouse rat. Even so, deep down, Deke didn't have much hope that they'd find Marty's brother, nor get him out if they did happen to stumble across him. "Probably get themselves killed," Deke muttered.

Besides the Utes, Tucker's men had to worry about the posse. Deke saw the tracks where three men broke away from the posse and followed Tucker. They kept their distance, never trying to close the gap.

Tossing his coffee on the fire, Deke decided to do something about the posse. He planned to lead them away from

Tucker and Marty. "If anybody kills him, it's gonna be me," Deke told his horse.

Three days later, Tucker's group first sighted Del Norte. They circled the town, always keeping below the horizon. Tucker led them to a small clearing and dismounted.

Even though they were less than two miles from town, the shoulder of a small mountain hid the town from view.

"You knew of this place," Marty accused, dismounting from her horse.

"In our business it pays to know good hiding places," Tucker admitted. "You boys set up camp. I'll ride into town with Miss Flynn and pick up some supplies and the money," Tucker instructed.

"Why can't we all go into town? I sure was looking forward to sleeping in a nice soft bed for a change," Danny complained.

"Why you lop-eared pup, don't you know we're wanted in Colorado," Weaver said, a trace of impatience in his voice.

"I ain't," Danny protested hotly.

Weaver jerked off his hat and whacked Danny across the shoulders with the brim. "You're with us, ain't you?" he asked, and Danny nodded sullenly. "Well, that's all it takes. So unless you want to get jerked out of that soft bed and end up being the belle of the ball at some necktie party, you'd best stay here."

"Boy, this outlaw business isn't as much fun as I thought it'd be," Danny said ruefully.

"You're too young to even know what fun is," Weaver told him. "Now get busy and unsaddle these horses, while I scout around a bit."

"I'll get Marty settled in the hotel and grab some supplies. I should be back before dark," Tucker told them.

Weaver stepped forward, his red face grave, as he wadded the brim of his hat in his hands. "Don't worry, Missy. We'll fetch your brother back, you can bet your bottom dollar on that."

For a second, Marty's face softened, and she looked like she would cry. All of a sudden, she threw her arms around Weaver, giving the outlaw a bear hug. "I know you will do your best," she said softly, then ran to where Tucker was waiting with the horses.

A tender expression on his weather-beaten face, Weaver balled up his hat, and scuffed the dirt. With a quick, almost angry gesture, he slapped his mashed hat on his head, and spun around. As he turned, Weaver saw the smirk on Danny's face. "Whadda you gawking at, boy? I thought I gave you a job to do. Now, get at it, 'fore I kick your worthless behind all over this camp," Weaver growled. Sniffling and wiping his nose on his sleeve, Weaver stole a glance back over his shoulder as Tucker and Marty rode away.

Riding side by side, they skirted the mountain and rode into town. For once Marty rode quiet, without her usual chitchat. Glancing sideways at her, Tucker watched her frown and fidget nervously in the saddle. Glad that she wasn't badgering him with a bunch of fool questions, Tucker didn't bother to question her strange behavior.

As soon as they turned down the wide, dusty street which split the town in half, Tucker sensed something was wrong. A throng of people milled about in the middle of the street. Some merely looked on, while others shouted and gestured wildly.

Pulling back on the reins, Tucker stopped his horse and slipped the thong off his pistol. Marty arched her eyebrows at the action. Tucker gave her a small shrug and touched a spur to the bay.

Tucker guided his horse up to the edge of the crowd. "What's all the excitement about?" he asked.

A small, slight-built man dressed in clean range clothes glanced up at the two figures on horseback. "Bank was robbed yesterday. The posse just got back."

"They catch the fellers that done it?" Tucker asked, more out of professional curiosity than anything else.

"Naw," the small man answered. "That's what's got folks so upset. They got near all the money in this whole town, which wasn't much."

Marty reached out and plucked Tucker's sleeve. "Let's go over to the restaurant and get a cup of coffee," she suggested.

"Alright," Tucker agreed with a shrug.

Together, they pulled the horses around and crossed the street to the cafe. A plump, middle-aged woman stood in the doorway of the cafe. She shielded her eyes, trying to see what was taking place across the street. She frowned as Tucker and Marty dismounted in front of the cafe. "You want something to eat?" she asked irritably.

"Not right now, just coffee," Marty replied cheerfully.

"Pot's on the stove. Help yourselves," the woman said, never taking her eyes off the crowd.

Marty and Tucker edged past her and into the cafe. The place was divided by a long counter. Behind it, dishes were stacked haphazardly on narrow shelves. The front half of the cafe was littered with tables and chairs scattered aimlessly about the room.

"Go ahead and grab a seat. I'll get the coffee," Tucker offered. Crossing behind the counter, Tucker poked around until he found two graniteware cups that looked reasonably clean. Filling them from the pot which sat on the huge stove, he joined Marty at the table.

"We've got a problem," Marty said, as soon as Tucker sat down.

"What kind of problem?" Tucker asked warily.

"The bank's been robbed," Marty explained patiently. "The money I was going to pay you and buy supplies with was in that bank!"

Tucker swore quickly, dropped his coffee cup, spilling some on the scarred tabletop. "You mean you're broke?" he demanded.

"Practically," Marty replied woefully. "I was thinking that perhaps you and your men could buy the supplies. I'm sure I could raise the money by the time you got back."

Tucker swore again, under his breath this time. "My brother has money. He's pretty well off," Marty added hastily.

"That ain't the problem, lady. We ain't got enough money between us to outfit a turkey shoot, much less an operation like this," Tucker grumbled. "Why do you think we stuck up that bank in Silver City?"

"Maybe we could raise some money here in town," Marty suggested hopefully.

"I don't see how," Tucker countered. "Somebody done had that idea," he said, gesturing to the crowd in the street.

Marty didn't say anything, but her lower lip quivered, and she looked about ready to cry. "Alright, alright, we'll go talk it over with the boys. Maybe we can work something," Tucker said, giving in.

He dug in his pocket and dropped a coin on the table beside the cups. Taking Marty's hand, they walked out the door.

"I left some money on the table for the coffee," Tucker told the lady in the doorway.

She glanced back at the table as if to make sure Tucker wasn't lying. "Look at them," she said irritably. "A bunch of fools and busybodies. I say let the sheriff handle this, but they just have to know everything that goes on."

Tucker chuckled at the lady's attitude. "They ain't like you. All business, I mean."

She grunted loudly and her hard eyes followed Tucker as he helped Marty on her horse. Tucker gave the waitress a huge smile as he swung aboard his own horse, but drew only a mad scowl in return.

As they rode from town, Tucker and Marty were being watched. The small man they spoke with earlier stared curiously at their retreating backs. He took off his hat, running a finger around the sweat band. Now, why in the world would anyone ride into town for just a cup of coffee?

The small man lived an ordered life and strange things bothered him. The actions of the pair seemed strangely out of place to him. Still bothered by the fact that a man and woman would ride into town just for coffee, the small man returned his attention to the posse.

"I heard Tucker was in the area. I bet his bunch was the ones that took our money," a young man wearing a deputy's star declared hotly. "I say we should go get our money back and string the whole bunch of them up!"

The young man's name was Delbert Gaines, and until now, no one in this town had paid any attention to him. Delbert's father owned a modest farm where Delbert worked. For the thousandth time, Delbert wished they had enough cattle to call the place a ranch.

This holdup, Delbert thought, was the best thing that ever happened to him. His chest swelled with pride. Since being asked to join the posse, Delbert felt he had the respect of the whole town. Delbert didn't stop to remember that every man who'd wanted to go had been welcomed. In Delbert's mind, he felt sure the sheriff asked him to come along because he was such a good shot and tracker. I'm probably as good with a gun as Tucker, Delbert told himself.

"It's as plain as a hog's nose who done this. Everybody knows it had to be Tucker. Let's quit stalling around and go get him!" Delbert repeated, puffing out his chest and hitching up his gunbelt.

"Maybe it was Tucker," the sheriff said tiredly. "Just how do you propose to find him?"

Delbert's face lost some of its glow as he frowned and puckered his brow. "I don't rightly know," he admitted. "But one thing I do know; Tucker ain't likely to ride up to this porch and give himself up."

The small man spun around to look in the direction Tucker and Marty had taken. "I don't know about that, kid," the small man said softly. He rubbed his hands together, a greedy smile playing on his lips.

Chapter Five

Weaver met Tucker and Marty at the edge of the camp. "That didn't take long," the big outlaw commented, looking curiously at Marty. "I wasn't looking for you to be back so soon."

"We've got a problem," Tucker replied gruffly. "Where's the others?"

"Hardy's back in the trees catching some shut-eye. I sent Danny down to the meadow with the horses. I figured they needed to graze a bit."

Tucker nodded absently, he wasn't worried about horses. Right now, money sat in the top drawer of his mind. "Shake Hardy awake, will you? We've gotta come up with a new plan."

Hardy heard them talking, and was already awake. "What happened in town?" he asked, watching Marty closely.

Tucker shrugged, disgust written all over his face. "Some fool went and stuck up the bank. They hoisted all of Marty's money. She ain't even got enough left to outfit us."

Hardy didn't have anything to say, but his eyes never left Marty. Weaver on the other hand groaned loudly, slapping his forehead. "I knew it! All of this ridin' and stirrin' around for nothing. I had a bad feeling about this deal all the time," he complained.

"Maybe not, Marty said her brother is well off and can pay the money if—" Tucker paused. "How much money have you guys got?"

37

Weaver groaned again. "You know I lost all of mine in that poker game."

"What about Danny?" Tucker asked quickly.

Weaver gave Tucker a blistering look. "Are you crazy? When did you ever know that kid to have money?"

Hardy pulled a twenty dollar gold piece from his pocket and tossed it to Tucker.

"Would that be enough to get an outfit together?" Marty asked, excitement shining in her eyes. "If you find my brother, he can get the ten thousand for you."

"I don't think so," Hardy said, quietly.

"What do you mean?" Tucker demanded, as Marty's face went white as a sheet.

"Your brother was Ben Flynn?" Hardy asked, and Marty nodded hesitantly. "I knew him. He is dead now."

Marty's face turned even paler and she looked at the ground. "What in blazes are you trying to say, Hardy?" Tucker asked harshly.

"Her brother did have a run-in with the Utes, that is true. He is dead now, I know this because I helped bury him. That was almost five years ago."

"Five years ago," Weaver sputtered, groaning again. "I tried to tell you, I said all along we was just wasting our time. Shoot, there ain't even a bank left to rob in these parts."

Hardy smiled, his strong, white teeth gleaming. "Tell them about the rest," he said to Marty. Marty face took on a pained expression, and her knuckles turned white. She set her jaw firmly, refusing to speak.

Hardy only chuckled and decided to tell the story for her. "Ben sure enough came into these mountains. I know cause I came with him. He let on like he was doing some exploring for the army, but that wasn't so. Fact was, he came looking for treasure. Well, not so much hunting for it, as going to pick it up.''

"Treasure?'' Weaver asked breathlessly.

Hardy nodded, pausing to roll a smoke. "Come on, man, get on with it,'' Weaver grumbled. "Tell us about the treasure.''

"Ben had a map, and a good one at that. I saw the map in Denver. Anyway, a week out of Denver, we was getting close to the treasure. I never knew exactly where the treasure was, I only saw the map for a second, I only know it was somewhere north and west of here. On the back of the map was a set of instructions.''

Hardy cupped his hands around the cigarette as he lit the end. He had everyone's attention now. Even a sore-looking Marty waited expectantly for him to continue.

"How did you know about the map?'' she asked, her face hard with suspicion.

"Like I said, we was in Denver, gathering supplies. Ben spread the word around that we was looking for some extra horses. One day, a man stops me on the street and says he has some horses for sale. He wanted Ben to come look at them.

"So, I went to Ben's room in the hotel. Ben wasn't there, but this map was spread out on the bed. I only looked at it for a second, before Ben came in and grabbed it. That's when I saw the directions on the back.''

"How did you know it was a treasure map?'' Marty demanded. "After all, one would come in handy on an exploration trip.''

"I didn't at first,'' Hardy admitted. "But I got to thinking about the directions on the back. If we were just exploring, why have directions to a certain spot. Then I remembered a spot on the map marked with an arrow.''

Marty wanted to ask another question, but Tucker cut her

off. "Let him tell the story. You can rake him over the coals later." When Hardy didn't speak up right away, Tucker prodded him. "Well, get on with it."

"When we was a week out of Denver, I figured we were getting real close to the treasure. Ben started acting jumpy and watching the landmarks real close. That was when the Utes hit us.

"They fired from the trees, we never even knew they was about. The first volley killed Ben and another feller. Caught out in one of those mountain meadows like we were, the only thing we could do was turn around and hightail it."

Hardy stopped and carefully snubbed out his smoke. Weaver took advantage of the delay to load up his pipe and lean back against a log.

"We scooted back into a stand of fir trees. From there we managed to beat them back. After the Utes left, we buried Ben and the other guy, then scrammed back to Denver," Hardy said. "I looked Ben over before we buried him. He didn't have the map on him," he added.

"Who else knew about the map?" Tucker asked, pacing the small camp like a caged wildcat.

"No one, except maybe Mason," Hardy replied, rolling himself another smoke.

"How can you be sure?" Weaver asked, around his pipe. "I mean any of the others could have found out about the map same as you did. What makes this Mason so special?"

"Mason was always poking into everything. He was the one that insisted we go back and bury Ben. He went through Ben's pockets, but he didn't find anything either. Of the six of us that made it out alive, he's the only one who stayed in this area."

"Are you sure of that?" Marty asked, and Hardy nodded. "That Mason, do you think he ever found the gold?"

"I doubt it. I kept track of him. He's never had much money." Hardy told her.

"So there is a treasure! Do you know where it is?" Tucker asked, as Weaver struggled to sit up.

"Of course there's a treasure," Marty snapped, irritated at having her thoughts interrupted. "I'm not sure exactly where it is, but I know the general area."

Weaver finally managed to sit up, dropping his pipe in his lap in the processes. "If we only had the map," he said wistfully. "Any idea where Ben could have cached it?" he asked, then suddenly became aware of the burning tobacco in his lap. With a yelp, the big outlaw bounded to his feet, frantically brushing the sparks from his pants.

Tucker turned away in disgust, kicking a rock across the clearing. "Aw, come on, Weaver. This isn't anything to get excited about," Tucker fumed.

"The heck you say," Weaver shouted. "I thought I was going to be riding side-saddle for quite a spell!"

Despite himself, Tucker had to laugh. "That wasn't what I meant, I was talking about the treasure. Without the map and good directions we could look forever."

Hardy nodded in agreement. That was exactly why he had never gone looking for the treasure, even though he knew approximately where to look.

Weaver's face fell and a hound dog expression crossed his face. "I'm afraid Tucker is right, ma'am. Without that map there just ain't any reason to go looking. You could look for a month of Sundays, and you'd never find anything."

Marty stood and slowly looked at each of the three men. Could she trust these men? "I'll make a deal with you," she began. "If you help me, I'll split whatever we find. Half for me, and half for you guys."

Tucker swore and turned away. "Are you deaf, lady?"

he shouted, turning back. "Without the map, we just won't find anything to split."

Marty smiled sweetly. "I have the map," she said smugly. "Ben memorized it, then mailed it to me from Denver. It tells exactly where to find ten million dollars worth of gold!"

Deke Carlin stared at the ground in disgust. What in the world was going on? The three posse members had followed Tucker into Colorado. Then instead of trying to arrest him, they passed him.

Deke trailed the posse for several miles. They circled wide around Tucker's camp, then took off like their tails were on fire.

For the life of him, Deke couldn't figure out their purpose. Something didn't smell right about the whole deal.

After wasting almost a full day trailing the three men from the posse, Deke came back to Tucker's trail to find that it had vanished.

Deke cut back and forth across the country, looking for Tucker's trail with no luck. Now, he stopped, trying to think things through.

Something fishy was going on here, and Deke intended to find out what it was. Even if he had to wring Tucker's fool neck to do it.

Chapter Six

"Ten million dollars!" Weaver shouted, tripping as he tried to climb to his feet. "Lordy! That's more money than a man could spend in a hunert years!"

"There might not be quite that much," Marty admitted. "Ben figured there was between a million and ten million dollars worth of gold and stones."

"How did your brother find out about this so-called treasure? Where did it come from?" Tucker asked, doubting her story.

"The treasure came from the mountains of Mexico," Marty answered quietly. "Ben found out about the gold in an old diary he found. Now, can we address ourselves to the problem of finding the necessary supplies?"

Tucker wanted to protest. The more he considered Marty's story, the less he believed. "We ain't moving until I get some answers. Some answers I can believe," Tucker stated, walking up to Marty and crossing his arms across his chest. "So far everything you've told us has been nothing but a pack of lies."

Marty didn't back down, instead she thrust out her jaw and glared right back at Tucker. "I never exactly lied, I just never explained all the facts. My brother did have a run-in with Indians," Marty said through clenched teeth. "If you knew where a fortune was hidden, would you tell the first pack of yokels you met, then sit back and hope

43

they shared?'' Marty asked, pushing her nose within inches of Tucker's face.

"Aw, come on, Tucker, go easy on her." Weaver urged quickly. "It ain't like you never stretched the truth."

"Weaver is right, for once," Hardy agreed.

Weaver shot Hardy a dark look, but remained silent. "I can tell you the rest of the story tonight." Marty urged, sensing a weakening in Tucker's position. "The important thing now is to get our supplies and some pack horses and get started."

"Alright," Tucker agreed. "I still don't see any need to hurry. That gold's been there a long time. A few more days ain't going to make any difference."

"The sooner we get the gold, the sooner we can start spending it," Weaver encouraged, rubbing his meaty hands together. "Besides, I don't like hanging around this close to town. What if some joker was to spot us?"

Weaver had a point. At any time they could be discovered. Discovery meant jail for them. "Let's wait until dark. Then we'll go into town and see what we can do about rounding up some horses and supplies," Tucker decided.

"Are we gonna steal some?" Weaver asked, eager to be going.

"I don't think so," Tucker replied. "Unless you want to lead a posse up to the gold."

For a second, Weaver looked crestfallen. "I guess you're right," he conceded. "Just how do you plan on getting everything we need?"

"I don't know yet," Tucker grumbled. Turning the problem over in his mind, Tucker walked over to a shade tree and sat down.

Marty watched Tucker, a worried frown on her pretty face. Should she have told them about the map?

"Don't worry, missy," Weaver said reassuringly. "Tucker'll think of something; he always does."

Weaver ran a hand over the stubble on his cheeks. "Whatever notion he comes up with, I sure hope it ain't legal. I might pick up some bad habits.

"Being righteous and upstanding is about the hardest habit to break," Weaver told her, his beefy face serious. "Why, I knew a man who was a real honest to goodness bad man. He stole more money than a wagonload of carpetbaggers. Then one day he up and did one thing right, and it ruined him for life."

Marty tore her eyes from Tucker to look quizzically at Weaver. "Oh sure, it happened," Weaver said in all seriousness. "This feller came on some folks broke down in the desert. Their hosses were played out, and they was out of water. Well, this feller pitched in and helped them out."

Weaver paused and looked skyward as he remembered. "After that this feller was ruined. Folks got to expecting him to always do the right thing. Last I heard of him, he was selling Bibles down in the Cherokee Nation."

"That's very interesting, Mister Weaver," Marty replied politely. "but I'm sure that could never happen to you."

A big grin split Weaver's face. "Well, I hope not, but still, a body can never be too careful."

Leaning back against the tree, Tucker closed his eyes and tried to think. How to acquire extra horses and enough grub to get into the mountains and back out?

Sensing someone watching him, Tucker opened his eyes. Hardy stood over him, wearing a curious expression. In a single fluid motion, Hardy squatted beside Tucker. Hardy pushed back his hat and picked up a twig from the ground.

"That feller Mason I was talking about," Hardy started, rolling the twig between his strong, brown fingers. When Tucker nodded, Hardy continued, "Be on the lookout for him when you go back to town. He won't like it if he finds out you are going up in the mountains.''

Tucker stared at Hardy, trying to see if the man was serious. "How much trouble can one man be?" Tucker asked, shrugging it off.

"Plenty," Hardy warned. "This man is very dangerous."

Tucker sat upright. If Hardy said the man was dangerous, then Tucker believed it. "What does this guy look like?"

"A very small man. He'd be about thirty now. Very small, but a lot stronger than he looks," Hardy replied. "He is a very quick amigo. The day the Utes attacked he got off two shots before I even got my gun out."

"You are just full of good news today," Tucker said with a laugh to cover his concern. "Is there anything else I should know?"

"Mason carries a knife as well. It is faster than the gun, I think. I saw him practicing in the woods one time."

Having spoke his piece, Hardy snapped the twig in two and tossed the pieces aside. Leaving Tucker, he gathered Tucker's and Marty's horses.

Tucker watched as Hardy led the horses to where Danny held the other mounts, then closed his eyes again. Marty paced the small campsite, stopping every little bit to glare at Tucker. "Humph," she said, crossing her arms and stomping her foot.

Weaver relaxed in the warm sunshine, mending a torn shirt. He chuckled at Marty. That girl was a fire-eater, alright.

The crowd in Del Norte slowly broke up. Chores had to be done. These people had endured hardship before, and over the years, they learned to take troubles as they came.

Slowly, they drifted to their farms, or into the saloon. All except for Sheriff Carithers.

The sheriff took his job seriously. He vowed silently not to rest until the thieves had been caught and the money returned. Walking like a man carrying a heavy weight, the sheriff trudged up to his tiny cabin. After a meal, he intended to get right back on the trail.

The small man Tucker spoke with earlier scanned the retreating crowd with watchful eyes. Finally, he spied the face he sought. "Delbert, could I speak with you for a minute?"

"Sure thing, Mister Mason," Delbert replied promptly.

"Let's go over to the saloon. I'll buy you a drink," Mason offered. He didn't bother to wait on a reply, instead he spun around, confident Delbert would follow.

Like a puppy, Delbert tagged along behind Mason. This was the first time Delbert had ever been invited to the saloon for a drink. Delbert had been inside the saloon a couple of times, but never stayed long. Pa didn't hold with drinking. Despite all of his swaggering and bragging, Delbert feared the old man. Even now, Delbert glanced about just to make certain his pa wasn't around.

Licking his lips, Delbert followed Mason through the batwing doors. Mason called loudly for a bottle and two glasses, then led Delbert to a corner table.

Pulling back a chair, Delbert looked around the crowded saloon. He felt a wave of pride. Mason was a respected man, even feared. Delbert felt it an honor to be with such a man.

Mason waited until the bartender brought the bottle and glasses. Placing a hand on the bottle, he leaned across the table. "How did you know Tucker was in this area?"

Slightly taken back by the intentness in Mason's voice, Delbert cleared his throat and dug at his collar.

"Three men stopped by my pa's farm the other day. They said Tucker robbed the bank in Silver City."

"How did they know Tucker was the one that did it?" Mason demanded fiercely.

"They caught up with him down in New Mexico," Delbert replied. "These fellers were deputies, just like me," Delbert added, fingering the star pinned to his thin chest.

Mason smiled thinly. This kid was all ego and no brains. "How come they didn't arrest Tucker and his bunch?"

"Like I said, they was down in New Mexico," Delbert announced, with growing confidence. "They couldn't arrest him, but they did get the money back."

"Oh well, Tucker's probably long gone. Likely he's halfway to old Mexico by now," Mason suggested.

"No, sir," Delbert corrected. "These men I talked to, they was looking for Tucker. They said he doubled back and came back this way. The tracked him for a ways, then lost the trail."

"Did they say if a dark-skinned man named Hardy was with Tucker?" Mason asked, his eyes blazing.

"I don't rightly recall, but the name sounds familiar. Hardy? Yeah, I think that was one of them."

Mason laughed and poured them both a drink. "I reckon you was right all along. Tucker surely was the one that robbed our bank," Mason agreed, sliding a drink across the table to Delbert.

Delbert took his glass, watching as Mason downed his drink in one gulp. Wrinkling his nose against the powerful aroma of the drink, Delbert tipped the glass to his lips. He couldn't get all the whiskey down in one gulp and had to swallow again. Tears sprang to his eyes, and Delbert coughed, but he kept the drink down.

Mason didn't seem to notice the trouble Delbert was having. The older man fished two cigars out of his vest.

The first he poked into his mouth and passed the second to his young companion. Digging in his pocket for a match, Mason grinned across the table. Snapping the match on his thumbnail, Mason lit his cigar. Leaning over, he held the flame under Delbert's cigar.

"I hear you are pretty good with a gun," Mason suggested, studying the flame.

"I get by," Delbert replied casually. "Nobody gives me any trouble."

"That's what I hear," Mason agreed, waving out the match. "How would you like to make some money?"

"What do you mean?" Delbert asked, taking the cigar from his mouth and holding it away from his body, as if it might explode. His stomach felt queasy and his head buzzed fiercely.

"I got a good idea where Tucker and his men might be hiding," Mason announced, smugly puffing his cigar. "Me and you could go capture them and get the money back for the bank. Of course there is a reward on Tucker, the others as well. Just think of it, we'd be famous!"

Delbert turned the idea over in his mind, liking the sound of it. The man who brought Tucker in! Man that was a feat. Unconsciously, Delbert rubbed the cold butt of his pistol. If they could pull this off, Delbert could finally get out from under his father's control. With the reward money he could leave Del Norte. Maybe he could go to Dodge.

"Okay, Mister Mason. I'll help you," Delbert said, trying to ignore the feeling of dread in the pit of his stomach. "When do we leave?"

"Right now," Mason answered, pouring them both another drink. "Drink up, then we'll leave."

Right now! Delbert looked around quickly, searching for a way out. Somehow, he hadn't thought they'd leave right then. Woodenly, Delbert finished his drink and followed Mason out to the horses.

Before mounting, Mason pulled his rifle from the boot and checked the loads. "Alright, kid, let's go get them," he said, snapping the breech closed.

Mechanically, Delbert mounted and followed. His head burned red hot, but his feet felt like blocks of ice in the stirrups.

Chapter Seven

Tucker woke with a start. He hadn't meant to sleep, but sitting in the shade made him drowsy. Glancing about, he saw Weaver stretched out asleep, snoring like a rusty pump organ. Hardy sat near him on a !og, cleaning his gun. Danny and Marty sat beside a small fire, talking in low tones. Stretching his arms, Tucker yawned mightily.

"It's about time you woke up. Did you dream up a brilliant plan?" Marty asked, her voice laced with sarcasm.

"Maybe," Tucker grunted, unwilling to admit he hadn't.

"Why don't we just steal some horses and go get the gold?" Danny asked, his young face shining eagerly.

Weaver sat up, rubbing his eyes. "What are you using for brains, boy?" Weaver asked. "You steal somebody's horses and they're gonna chase you. Do you want to lead a whole passel of folks up to our treasure?"

"I guess not," Danny mumbled, some of his enthusiasm gone.

"I should say not!" Weaver scolded, clapping the youngster across the shoulders. "Now, you just keep your trap shut, while us older folks decide what's best."

Danny walked to the edge of the clearing, muttering to himself. "One of these days, that boy is going to shoot you," Hardy warned.

"Naw," Weaver replied with a chuckle. "I'm just funning him. Besides, the boy's got to learn sometime."

51

"How many horses are we going to need to carry this treasure?" Tucker cut in with his question.

"The diary talks of ten strong men carrying it," Marty replied.

"We'll have to get our hands on at least four pack horses," Tucker decided.

"That won't be necessary," a strong voice cut in from the edge of the trees. "Now, one at a time drop your guns. Tucker, you go first."

Cursing himself for being careless, Tucker slowly undid the buckle on his gunbelt. They should have kept a watch. All this talk of treasure made them sloppy.

As the buckle came loose, Tucker considered making a try for his gun. He felt his men watching him, ready to back any play he made. The trouble was that Tucker didn't know how many men were out there, or even where they were. With a sigh, Tucker let his gunbelt fall.

"That was very smart. Now kick it away from you," the unknown voice instructed. "Alright, Hardy, toss your pistol beside it."

Hardy didn't even hesitate. He'd been cleaning his gun, and the weapon was empty and useless. As Hardy's pistol thudded to the ground, a small man stepped from behind the trees. He held a rifle, loosely pointed at the group.

"Okay, you," he said, pointing the rifle directly at Weaver. "Drop your gunbelt and kick it over by the others."

Weaver swore bitterly under his breath, but began working on his buckle with careful fingers. As the belt slid down Weaver's hips, a scared-looking youngster stepped up beside Mason. Sweat rolled down his cheeks as he held his gun with both hands, looking frightened enough to drop the weapon.

Danny stood off to one side, watching the whole proceeding. He couldn't believe that his friends were going to just give up their guns and surrender. His palms sweating, Danny tried to calculate his chances of getting his gun out and rescuing his friends. Just then, Mason's eyes flicked to Danny.

For an instant, Danny's heart almost stopped, sure that Mason guessed what Danny was thinking. Then Mason's eyes swung back to Weaver. Just as Weaver's gunbelt landed in the pile with the others, Danny decided to make his move. Sucking in a deep breath, Danny dropped his hand to his gun.

Mason heard the sharp intake of breath and saw the blur of movement out of the corner of his eye. Pivoting with incredible swiftness, he swung his rifle and fired. The bullet spun Danny around, knocking him flat on the ground.

Quick as a wink, he swung his rifle back to cover the others. Weaver had started for Mason, but stopped dead in his tracks. Clenching his fist, Weaver stared at Mason, anguish written all over the big man's face.

"Easy, big man," Mason warned, jacking another shell into the chamber. "I don't want to kill you; not just yet anyway."

Shaking all over, Weaver growled in helpless rage. Mason gave the big man a cocky sneer and said, "Delbert, get the kid's gun and put it in the pile with the others."

Delbert jumped at the sound of his own name. He turned large frightened eyes to Mason. Mason motioned for him to get the gun. Walking stiffly and slowly, Delbert went to Danny and took the pistol from his limp hand. As soon as Delbert had the gun, Mason visibly relaxed.

"Well, well, Hardy, I always figured you'd be back for the gold. It sure took you a long time to work up your courage. Did you think you would be safe if you brought this loudmouth with you?'' Mason asked, waving his rifle at Tucker.

Hardy sat in silence, his face emotionless. Only his eyes showed any feeling. They glared fiercely at Mason.

"Nothing to say, huh," Mason said with a shrug. "I always did figure that you made off with the map. I shoulda killed you then, but I wasn't sure."

Mason pointed the rifle squarely at Hardy's forehead. "Now, give me the map." When Hardy didn't say anything, Mason leaned forward, pressing the muzzle of the rifle against the man's copper-tinged cheek. "I can always take it off your body," Mason said, his voice so soft that even in the stillness of the clearing it could barely be heard.

"He hasn't got the map. I do," Marty spoke up.

Mason kept the rifle against Hardy's cheek as he looked past Tucker to Marty. "And who might you be?" he asked.

"Martha Flynn," Marty replied with quiet dignity. "Ben mailed me the map before he left Denver."

Mason laughed, stepping away from Hardy. "Ole Ben, he always was a cagey one. He never trusted nobody. Now, give me the map."

Trying to look dejected, Marty opened her small clutch purse and reached inside. Instead of pulling out the map, she jerked out a tiny derringer. Marty jerked the gun free from the purse and fired both shots as fast as she could.

Tucker had been watching Mason, waiting for a chance, when the shots rang out. At the same instant he heard the shots, Tucker felt a searing pain in his backside. Marty's second bullet hit Delbert in the lower leg, dropping him in a heap beside Danny.

While Mason's attention was on Marty, Hardy's hand swept to his boot top and the knife he kept there. Pulling the knife free, he flipped it underhanded at Mason.

Mason saw the deadly knife coming and managed to twist

out of the way. Dodging the knife, Mason lost his balance and slipped down to one knee.

Before Mason could recover, Weaver dove on top of him. With one swipe of his big hand Weaver slapped the rifle from Mason's hands. Closing his hands around Mason's scrawny neck, Weaver lifted the smaller man bodily from the ground, slamming him backwards into a tree. Mason bounced off of the tree like a rag doll, a trickle of blood running down his face. As Mason teetered on his feet, Weaver drove his fist into the smaller man's face. Mason's feet left the ground, and he landed flat on his shoulders. He tried to get up, then fell back and lay still.

Hardy snatched up Mason's fallen rifle and stepped back so he could cover the whole area. For a long time the only sound was the heavy breathing of Weaver.

Marty covered her mouth with her hand, as she stared at the scene in horror. Four men lay on the ground, each of them as still as death.

Deke Carlin rode slowly into Del Norte. He watched closely for signs of Marty Flynn or Tucker's gang. Three days ago, Deke lost their trail and never found it again. Del Norte seemed the logical place for them to get supplies, so Deke went there.

Deke dismounted in front of the cafe. Tying his horse to the hitching rail, Deke's eyes scanned the town carefully, but saw no signs of those he pursued.

Giving his horse a pat, he ducked under the hitching rail, and went in the cafe. A sour-looking woman looked up from a month-old newspaper to scowl at Deke.

"You want something to eat?" she challenged.

"Whatever you got," Deke answered, dropping into a chair.

The woman grunted harshly, crossing to the stove. Steam

rolled out of the pot as she opened the lid. Searching the counter, she found a bowl and filled it with beans from the pot. She broke a chunk off a moldy loaf of bread and tossed it on top of the beans.

"You want coffee?" she asked, slamming the bowl down in front of Deke.

"Please," Deke said, hoping she wouldn't refuse. The lady wasn't happy, but she went back to the stove. "This seems like a nice little town," Deke offered, trying to make conversation.

"It used to be, I suppose," the waitress answered. "Then some fool went and robbed the bank."

Deke Carlin's hand froze halfway to his mouth with a spoonload of beans. "You say the bank was robbed? They know who did it?"

The waitress shrugged. "The law we have in these parts couldn't catch a drunk horse thief in a dead-end alley," she supplied. "Word around town is that Tucker Evans done it."

Deke cursed bitterly to himself. "Course they'll never catch him," the waitress said, finally finding a subject she liked. "We're just out our money. The men in this town ain't got the smarts to catch a man like Tucker. Even if they knew where to find him, they wouldn't have the gumption to go get him."

Deke ignored the woman's rantings. His face set in grim lines, he pushed his meal away. Tucker had been warned, no funny business with Marty. Now he had gotten her involved in a bank heist.

Deke had promised to kill Tucker if he didn't treat Marty right, now Deke intended to keep that promise!

Chapter Eight

Weaver rushed over to where Danny fell. Dropping beside the fallen youngster, Weaver gently rolled Danny over. Sniffling, Weaver gently brushed the dirt from Danny's face. Danny cautiously opened one eye. When he saw that it was Weaver standing over him, the boy broke into a smile.

Weaver saw the smile and blew his top. "Boy you scared me half to death. Don't ever try and pull a stupid stunt like that again!"

"Don't worry, I won't," Danny promised, trying to move his left arm. Immediately, the smile vanished and was replaced by a grimace of pain.

"Let me look at that arm," Weaver said gruffly. His tone was rough, but his hands were gentle as he pulled back the shirt-sleeve so he could see the wound. "That's not so bad, I'll have you up and in perfect shape in no time.

"You don't go nowhere, I'll get my doctoring tools and be right back," Weaver instructed, laboring as he climbed to his feet.

Assured that Danny was going to be alright, Weaver looked to the other wounded men. Tucker was on his hands and knees cursing steadily, and very fluently.

"You gonna live, Tucker?" Weaver asked, bending down to look at Delbert Gaines's leg.

Tucker ignored Weaver's question, asking one of his own. "How's Danny?"

Weaver waved off Tucker's concerns. "Aw, he'll be fine. The bullet went through the meat on the inside of his arm. Why, I've had worse injuries just doing a good day's work."

"When did you ever do a day's work—good or otherwise?" Hardy asked derisively.

Weaver shot Hardy a dark look, but ignored the comment, returning to his work. "I'll have to take the boot off to see the wound. It may hurt just a bit," Weaver said gently.

Delbert nodded, his face pale and his lower lip trembling. Weaver took the boot in his hands, looking Delbert in the eyes. With a quick jerk, Weaver pulled the boot off. Delbert sucked in a deep breath and his whole body arched.

"That's the best way. Just get it over with," Weaver said. From the pained expression on his smooth face, Delbert clearly did not agree with that strategy.

Weaver pushed up the boy's pant leg, which was already soaked with blood. The bullet had glanced off the shin bone and ranged down, taking a chunk out of the side of Delbert's foot.

"That's gonna be sore as a boil, but nothing's broken," Weaver told Delbert. "Where did you get hit?" he asked Tucker, who was still on his hands and knees.

"Right in the business end," Hardy answered, leaning around to look at Tucker's backside.

"I'll be alright, you go ahead and fix up the young'ns," Tucker growled, his lips set tight against the pain.

"You're the boss," Weaver replied, with a shrug. "I got a bottle of red-eye in my saddle bag. You want to fetch it for me?" Weaver asked, looking at Marty.

Marty nodded slowly. She was still in shock over what had happened, and the fact that she caused most of it. She brought the whole saddlebag to Weaver.

Weaver took the bag from her, eyeing her wooden expression curiously. "Don't worry, Missy, everyone's gonna live," he assured. Marty gave him a quick grateful smile, as she knelt beside him to help.

"Here, boy, take a snort of this," Weaver said, digging a bottle from the saddlebag and tossing it up to Delbert. "We'll do part of the healing from the inside out." Weaver told him.

Delbert took a small drink and started to hand the bottle back. Changing his mind, Delbert took another drink, a big one this time.

Weaver nodded approvingly. "Thata boy," he said, then took the bottle. He splashed some of the whiskey on Delbert's leg and foot. Delbert sniffled and drug his sleeve across his nose, bracing himself for what was coming next.

"Don't fret, the worst is done," Weaver predicted.

He took an old shirt from his bag and ripped it into long strips. He folded one of the strips into a pad and placed it against Delbert's injured foot. Marty held the pad in place, while Weaver used another strip to tie it. He looked critically at the gash on Delbert's shin.

"That ain't bleeding too bad, I don't think it needs a bandage," he decided. "It'll probably swell up like a bullfrog on a hot day though." He handed the bottle back to Delbert. "Better have another shot of this tarantula juice. It'll keep you from getting the distemper while you're healing."

After Delbert finished drinking Weaver passed the bottle to Danny. "When you was lying there on the ground, why didn't you let me know you was still alive? I was scared we'd lost you." Weaver asked Danny.

"I was afraid if I moved, he'd shoot me again," Danny answered ruefully.

"Lucky for you that you was on the ground when ole

deadeye Marty opened up with her toy cannon," Tucker commented, limping to the pile of guns.

"I'm sorry," Marty said sincerely. "The gun went off before I was ready. I haven't shot a gun much."

"No kidding," Tucker mumbled, picking his gun and belt from the pile. "Shoot, I thought you was an expert."

"Aw, quit your bellyaching, she pulled our fat out of the fire," Weaver commented, as he wound a bandage around Danny's arm. He tied the bandage off, then cuffed Danny alongside the head.

"Hey! What was that for?" Danny protested.

"That was for almost getting yourself kilt. Don't ever do that again. My back is still aching from burying them fellers the other day, planting you'd likely do me in."

Mason started to stir as Weaver finished up on Danny. Mason groaned and felt the skinned spot on his head. Groaning again, he rolled over and sat up. His eyes found Hardy and the rifle he held, and he froze. Slowly he began to rub his forehead, working his way around to the back of his head.

"Looking for this?" Hardy asked, holding up the slim-bladed throwing knife he'd taken from the scabbard behind Mason's neck. "What do you want to do with him?" Hardy asked Tucker.

"Tie him up," Tucker replied shortly. "Weaver, haul your rear end over here before I bleed to death," Tucker hollered.

Weaver lumbered over to where Tucker lay on the ground. "Roll over on your belly so I can get a look at it," Weaver instructed. "And quit your griping, you'll have to take your medicine like the rest of them," Weaver added gruffly, when Tucker started to protest.

Tucker took the big outlaw's scolding and rolled meekly

onto his stomach. "How bad is it?" Tucker asked, craning his neck to see.

For an answer, Weaver threw back his head and laughed, his booming laughter filling the small clearing. "It be more embarrassing than anything," Weaver chortled. "Now skin outta them britches so I can get down to business."

"Do you need any help, Mister Weaver?" Marty asked from across the clearing.

"No, he does not!" Tucker snapped, and Weaver chuckled. "Hardy, go find their horses, and take her with you."

Silently, Hardy left the clearing with a solemn-faced Marty in tow. As soon as they were out of sight, Tucker heard Marty's laughter start. He could even imagine hearing a low chuckle from the taciturn Hardy.

"Oh man, I ain't never gonna live this down," Tucker moaned, slipping out of his jeans.

"Living it down ain't gonna be the problem," Weaver told him. "Sitting down is going to the trouble. Your saddle ain't gonna fit right for a few days."

Looking back over his shoulder, Tucker could see Weaver's big chest heaving and his face turning beet red, as he tried to control his mirth. "Weaver, I swear, if you laugh one more time, I gonna bend this six-gun over your skull," Tucker threatened.

Weaver tactfully chose to remain silent as he worked. Every once in a while a snort would escape past his compressed lips, and Tucker's ears would turn red.

"The bullet passed clean through. It chewed up some hide and meat, but that's about it. This would heal a lot faster if we cut a hole in the seat of your britches to let the air circulate through."

Tucker saw Mason struggling against his bonds. Snatching up his pistol, Tucker pointed the gun at Mason. "You just sit still. I blame you for this, and I wouldn't need much of an excuse to let the air circulate through you," Tucker threatened, cocking the revolver as he spoke.

Mason's face turned dark, and his lips thinned down, but he quit pulling against his bonds. "You can't keep me tied up forever. Sooner or later I'll get loose."

"Maybe you're right," Tucker acknowledged, some of his good humor returning, as he watched someone else suffer. "I may not be able to keep you hog tied forever, but I can put a bullet in your brisket, that'll keep you quiet."

"All finished," Weaver decided, stepping back to admire his handiwork. "I won't say you're as good as new, but I reckon you'll get by," he added, casting about for Tucker's bedroll.

He let out a grunt as he spotted it by the fire. He fished out a pair of pants and tossed them to Tucker. "What are you planning on doing with these two?" the big outlaw asked, patting his pockets for his pipe.

Tucker eased his legs in the jeans before answering. "I don't rightly know. Shoot them, I reckon."

Mason growled and spit in disgust. He felt certain that Tucker wouldn't just up and shoot them. Delbert didn't share his certainty. He shrank back, his lower lip trembling.

"Oh sure, shooting them is 'bout the only thing we could do. Say, why don't you let me have the boy? I sure need to sight in my Sharpes buffalo gun."

Tucker grimaced and nodded as he slid the jeans over his hips. Sweat poured off his face as he hitched them into place and buttoned them up. A huge sigh escaped his lips after he finished.

Weaver walked toward Delbert, cocking his head as he looked the boy over carefully. "He's a skinny youngster, but that's just what you need to sight in one of those big guns," Weaver said, taking a couple of steps closer to

Delbert. "You ever see a man get shot with a buffalo gun, boy?"

Delbert drew back and shook his head quickly. He flinched as Weaver laughed harshly.

"It's something, alright," Weaver told him. "It sounds like the butt end of an ax hitting an oak tree. I've seen one of them big slugs knock a full grown man back ten feet. A scrawny boy like yourself? Why it'd probably just tear you plumb in two."

Delbert whimpered softly, the color draining from his face. Biting his lip, he tried to tear his eyes from Weaver's whiskered face.

Hardy broke the tension as he and Marty led two horses into the clearing. One of them was a tall rangy bay, the other a scrubby pinto with a mangy-looking coat.

"Here's two of the horses we need. Now, if we can just find a couple of more, we'll be set," Marty said, holding the reins up proudly.

"We already found everything we need," Tucker corrected, moving stiffly to the fire. "You said this Mason has a ranch?" he asked Hardy.

"Yeah, but I don't know where it is," Hardy replied.

"He does," Tucker said, pointing at Mason. Mason stared at Tucker, eyes gleaming with hatred.

Chapter Nine

Weaver rode ahead, leading the bedraggled-looking bunch as they made their way to Mason's ranch. Hardy dropped back, covering their backtrail and keeping a watch behind them.

Tucker stood in the stirrups, trying to find a bearable way to sit in the saddle. Despite his discomfort, Tucker kept his rifle trained on Mason, who sulked in his saddle.

Tucker didn't pay much attention to Delbert. Both Delbert and Danny rode listlessly, their heads hanging. Neither paid any attention to what was going on around them.

Every time he looked at Delbert, Tucker felt ashamed. They'd scared the boy into telling them the location of Mason's ranch.

Marty steered her horse up beside Tucker's. "Would you like me to fold a blanket up for you to sit on?" she asked, and Tucker grunted no. "When we get to Mister Mason's ranch, I'll make a pillow for you to sit on. After all, it's the least I can do."

"I don't need no pillow," Tucker replied sourly. "Do you still have that little cannon?"

"Yes, it's in my clutch," Marty answered.

"Give it to me. It ain't safe around here as long as you're packing that durn thing," Tucker said, holding out his hand.

"I will not!" Marty exclaimed. "That gun was a gift from my brother. It's one of the only things I have left that he gave me."

"Except the map," Tucker replied dryly, and Marty nodded. "Alright, you can keep the gun, but keep it in your handbag from now on."

Mason, thinking that Tucker's attention was diverted, worked his hands around to grab his reins. Tucker leaned forward and whacked Mason solidly in the ribs with the rifle. "Settle down, or I'll tie you hand and foot and sling you across the saddle," Tucker threatened.

Without thinking, Tucker sat down in his saddle. "Yeow!" he yelled, jerking to a standing position again.

Marty snickered, covering her mouth with a gloved hand. "I'm sorry, Tucker, I didn't mean to laugh, I just couldn't help it."

For a moment, Marty turned serious. She touched Tucker's arm lightly, and a softness came into her eyes. "I am so sorry that I shot you. It was an accident. I'd never used a gun before, and it went off before I knew it."

All of a sudden, Tucker felt like a heel for all the griping and grumbling he'd done. "Aw, I'll be alright," he replied gruffly.

Marty smiled, and her eyes grew misty. "I know you will, but I still feel terrible about it," she said, and Tucker felt his face grow hot. Ducking his head, he studied his horse's ears.

"I'm also sorry that I didn't trust you and your men at first," Marty apologized, her face looking sad. "It's just that the treasure is all I've got in the world. If I were to lose it . . . well, I just don't know what I'd do."

"Don't you worry, we'll get that treasure for you," Tucker promised, his voice husky. Coughing, Tucker glanced around nervously. He saw Mason staring at him with a sneer on his face. Tucker jabbed him in the ribs with the rifle. "You jest keep looking straight ahead."

Marty's hand resting on his forearm gave Tucker a curious

thrill of excitement. It also made him nervous and jumpy. "Weaver, what are you doing up there?" Tucker bellowed, eager to be moving.

"Sorry, boss," Weaver called back, sounding not at all sorry. "I just figured it'd be easier on them boys if we took it slow and easy."

Tucker frowned, knowing Weaver was right, but eager to go faster. One look at Danny and Delbert told Tucker that anything faster than a walk was too fast.

Danny rode head down and hunched over in the saddle. He held the reins slackly in his good hand. Delbert, his bad leg dangling loosely, had his reins draped over his horse's neck. The youngster held on to the saddle horn with both hands.

Shaking his head at the delay, Tucker eased back and tried to sit in the saddle. Immediately, his backside felt a branding iron had been slapped against it. Gritting his teeth, Tucker tried to shift his weight, holding his injured side high. This put a kink in his side, but gave his legs a rest.

In spite of herself, Marty snickered at Tucker's discomfort, but she quickly covered her mouth with her hand as Tucker shot her a searing glancing. "I'm sorry, but you do look funny riding that way," Marty said.

Tucker ignored her, looking straight ahead. "You know you could walk," she offered.

Tucker glanced over at Marty like he thought she was crazy. "Why in the world would I want to do that?" He asked, shaking his head. Why in the world anyone would walk when there was a horse to ride was beyond him.

"A little walking never killed anyone," Marty pointed out. "Why, it might even do you some good."

Ignoring her, Tucker concentrated on the route they took. Staying under cover, they traveled just along the edge of the mountains. Through a break in the trees, he could see the vast expanse of the San Luis Valley. They rode on the western end of the valley, circling around to the north. It would have been closer to Mason's ranch if they had simply cut straight across the valley. None of them, however, cared to be out in the open that long.

Glancing back behind him, Tucker saw Hardy closing in from the rear. The outlaw slowed his horse, motioning for Tucker to drop back.

"Keep your eyes on those two," Tucker told Marty, "I'm gonna drop back and talk to Hardy."

Tucker caught the calculating gleam as it leaped into Mason's eyes. "Don't get any fancy notions, I'll still have you in my sights," Tucker told him, holding the rifle up for Mason to see.

Tucker pulled his horse aside, and let the others pull away. He wanted a smoke, but between standing in the stirrups and keeping his rifle trained on Mason, Tucker wasn't in a good position to roll one.

Hardy pulled alongside and began building himself a smoke. When he finished, Tucker reached out and plucked the cigarette from Hardy's brown fingers. "Thanks, I've been needing one of these. Now what's on your mind?" Tucker asked.

Hardy built himself another smoke and lit both his and Tucker's before answering. "I came across the trail of three men," Hardy said, exhaling blue smoke in enjoyment. "Like us, they circle the valley, keeping out of sight."

"I didn't see any tracks," Tucker objected.

Hardy took his cigarette from his mouth and chuckled. "You ain't in a good position to see the ground," Hardy replied, looking at the funny way Tucker rode. "We did not cross their trail, so you wouldn't have seen the tracks. These men were in the posse we saw in New Mexico."

Tucker jerked the cigarette from his mouth and stabbed

it out on his saddle horn. "I thought you said they never followed us," Tucker pointed out angrily.

"They aren't following us," Hardy said evenly. "They are ahead of us. They were moving fast, but they took pains to hide their trail."

Tucker tipped the rifle back over his shoulder, rubbing the side of his head with the barrel. "That don't make any sense at all," he mused, and Hardy shrugged. "Why don't you see if you can pick up their trail and find out where they are headed?" Tucker asked.

Without a word, Hardy swung his horse away. Watching the man ride away, Tucker wondered if he had hurt Hardy's feelings. Tucker hadn't meant to sound as if he doubted the man. If Hardy said the riders were from that posse, then Tucker whole-heartedly believed it. Hardy didn't make mistakes like that.

What would bring these men from the posse here? Why were they worried about being seen? Rubbing his jaw, Tucker saw Mason glance back for the third time in less than a minute. Pointing his finger like a pistol at Mason, Tucker squeezed off an imaginary shot.

Tucker realized that something had to be done with Mason. The man was relentless in his watching for a chance to escape. Hardy had been right, this was a very dangerous man.

Dismissing the problem from his mind, Tucker lifted his horse into a trot. Just a few seconds of trotting convinced Tucker that the pace Weaver had been setting was the right one. Every little bit, Tucker's backside would graze the saddle, sending jolts of pain through him.

"What was that all about?" Marty asked after Tucker caught up. "Nothing serious, I hope."

Tucker had been holding his breath against the pain, and

had to take a minute to get his breath back. "Nothing much. Hardy saw some tracks. He's going to check them out."

Marty didn't say anything, but she looked back nervously. "Don't worry. Hardy will find them," Tucker assured.

The shadows were beginning to grow long, when Weaver turned up the canyon leading to Mason's ranch. A mile or so up the canyon, they found Mason's ranch house situated under an overhang of the canyon wall. A small, swift running mountain stream flowed down the center of the canyon floor.

"I'll take care of the horses, if you want to get everyone inside and settled," Weaver offered.

"You might help us get these youngsters down first," Tucker replied.

Tucker dismounted, limped up to Mason's horse and grabbed the smaller man by the shirt collar. "Time to get down and go in. It's so nice of you to have us all over like this," Tucker said cheerfully, and pulled Mason from his horse. Tucker kept his hold on Mason's shirt, breaking his fall a little.

"Sorry about that. I musta slipped," Tucker apologized, sounding anything but sorry. Tightening his hold on Mason's shirt, he jerked the smaller man to his feet. Mason's eyes blazed with fury, as Tucker slung him up against the horse.

Tucker drew his knife and sliced the bonds holding the man's wrists. "Help Weaver get them boys down," Tucker instructed, spinning Mason around and giving him a healthy shove in the back.

Weaver already had Danny down, and Marty was helping the youngster into the house. It took both Weaver and Mason working together to get Delbert off his mount.

Once, they bumped Delbert's injured leg. Delbert's face turned ghastly white and he screwed his eyes shut, but not a sound escaped his lips. Once on the ground, Mason slipped an arm around Delbert's waist and helped him into the cabin.

Tucker followed them up to the house, while Weaver gathered the horses. Before entering the cabin, Tucker shaded his eyes and scanned their back trail for Hardy. In the bright red glow of the sunset, Tucker could find no sign of the man.

A perplexed frown on his face, Tucker pushed the door open with his rifle and stepped inside. The cabin looked larger from the inside than it did from outdoors. Two bunks, stacked one on top of the other, sat against the far wall. In one corner stood a huge stove and set of cupboards. A large washbasin sat on a table beside the back door. The middle of the room was bare, giving the cabin a bigger look.

Marty already had Danny in the upper bunk, and Mason was easing Delbert into the lower one. Both lads collapsed in their bunks, wore out from the long day's ride.

After checking to make sure the boys were comfortable, Tucker pulled a chair from under the table. Motioning for Mason to sit in the chair, Tucker glanced about the room for something to tie the smaller man with.

Spying a rope hanging from a peg in the wall, Tucker stretched out his rifle and fished it over to him. Using the whole twenty feet of rope, Tucker cinched Mason into the chair. Weaver entered the room just as Tucker finished. The big outlaw looked questioningly at the elaborate way Mason was tied. "I don't trust him," Tucker replied to the unspoken question.

"What's to eat?" Weaver asked, noticing that Marty was puttering around the stove.

"I don't know yet, I'm still looking," Marty replied cheerfully. "He sure has a lot of supplies here."

"Enough to get us into the mountains, and back out again?" Tucker asked, his interest piquing.

"Boy, I'd say so," Weaver declared, inspecting the contents of the cupboard over Marty's shoulder. "We'll eat good, too."

"Looks like you're used to that," Marty said, tapping Weaver's ample stomach with her finger.

"It helps me shed rainwater," Weaver agreed, giving Marty a big grin and a wink.

"Now, you two get out of here, so I can start cooking," Marty told them, shooing them away with her hands.

"Where are we supposed to go?" Tucker asked dubiously, looking around the tiny cabin.

"Oh, I don't know, but I can't have you looking over my shoulder while I cook."

"Can I help you get a fire started?" Weaver asked, sounding hopeful.

Marty glanced in the stove. "No thank you, Mister Weaver. The wood's already laid in. I believe I can manage from there."

The men retreated to the far side of the room, Weaver dragging a block of wood from the wood pile. "You want something to sit on?" he asked, plopping his backside down on the block.

"No, I believe I'll just stand," Tucker replied curtly, not quite sure if Weaver was making fun of him or not. "Are there any more horses on this place."

Weaver showed his teeth in a big smile. "You bet. There's a corral down by the stream. I even saw a couple of pack saddles."

"You don't mind if we use them?" Tucker asked Mason. "Well, of course you don't. You're such a hospitable man," Tucker said, before Mason could growl his surly reply.

They could hear soft hoofbeats on the hard-packed yard. Weaver shot off his block with amazing speed and agility for a man of his bulk. Tucker, moving slower because of his injury, reached the window a step behind his big friend.

"Who's out there?" Tucker asked, trying to look around Weaver's bulky shoulders.

"Relax. It's only Hardy," Weaver announced, sliding his pistol back in the scabbard. Tucker realized that he too was holding his gun. Shoving the pistol back in the holster, Tucker tried to remember when he had drawn it.

Weaver stepped back from the window, and Tucker stepped up. He watched Hardy lead the horse off in the direction of the corral. When Hardy reappeared out of the dark, Tucker smiled. The outlaw had circled around the cabin, approaching from the other side, just as Tucker knew he would. Hardy lived as wary as a wild animal.

Hardy would never think of entering any building before circling it. This carefulness had kept him alive, and the rest of the gang as well. Hardy's caution helped to offset Tucker's natural boldness.

Tucker limped to the door, and opened it for Hardy. "You find anything?"

"They headed deep back in the mountains. I trailed them quite a ways just to make sure they didn't decide to double back," Hardy explained. "Looked like they was looking for a place to hole up. Towards the end they was going real slow and taking more pains to hide their trail."

"What the Sam Hill are you two blabbering about? I didn't see any riders," Weaver demanded.

Irritated at the interruption, Tucker quickly explained the situation to Weaver. "You sure they wasn't looking for us?" he asked, after finishing the story.

"Sounds more like they was on the dodge from something," Weaver offered, looking to Hardy for confirmation.

Hardy only grunted and shrugged, as he went to the washbasin to clean the dirt and sweat from his face.

"I don't care who they are and what they are up to as long as they ain't looking for us," Tucker decided, dismissing the matter from his mind.

Hardy finished washing and tossed the dirty water out the back door. As he placed the basin back on the table, Hardy saw Marty laying out some dried apples. "A pie?" he questioned.

"I got ambitious," Marty explained, turning to give him a flashing smile. "You go sit with the others while I finish up."

Hardy crossed the room, looking curiously at the tightly bound Mason. The dark outlaw squatted beside Weaver, leaning his back against the rough logs of the wall. "Let's hole up here for a few days, let everyone heal up some," Hardy suggested.

Tucker thought it over for a minute, then agreed. "Might as well, I don't think the gold is going anywhere."

"It's ready," Marty called, piling a various assortment of pots and pans on the table. She dished up a plate apiece for Danny and Delbert before letting the others start.

As usual, Weaver was the first in line. He spooned beans and several strips of bacon on his plate. Looking at the plate, he decided it would hold more, so he had another go at the beans. Looking over the plate containing the rolls, he snatched up the two biggest.

After they had eaten, Marty pulled a pie from the oven. Weaver's eyes got big and, holding his plate out, he jumped for the pie.

Marty raised her hand, stopping him. "Someone should feed him," she said, nodding her head in Mason's direction.

"He don't get no pie, does he?" Weaver asked hurriedly.

"I'll feed him," Tucker said. "But be sure and save me a piece of that pie."

Tucker filled a plate for Mason, and carried it to him.

Tucker started to feed Mason, but then changed his mind. "I'm gonna let you feed yourself, but if you try anything funny, I'll bend my pistol over your head."

Mason waited patiently while Tucker untied him. "You'll never get the treasure and get out of the mountains alive. I'll see to that!" Mason threatened, as he took the plate from Tucker's hands.

"How do you know that I won't just shoot you before we leave?"

Mason looked over his plate, his lips curling in a sneer. "You don't have the guts. Pretty soon I'll get loose, and I promise you that you will die real slow!"

Chapter Ten

For three days, they rested at Mason's cabin. Tucker prowled the tiny space, feeling miserable during the long wait. Even though his wound still bothered him, he was eager to be moving. Despite his earlier scoffings at the possibility of finding the gold, the treasure bug had bit Tucker.

After supper on the third night, Tucker helped Marty clear away the dishes. Even though they planned to leave before daylight the next day, Marty insisted on washing the dishes.

For the life of him, Tucker couldn't see the logic in that. "We ain't gonna use these again, no sense in bothering to wash them," he reasoned.

"I don't like leaving a mess," Marty replied, as if that explained everything.

"Leave a mess? For Mason, who cares?" Tucker argued. "I'd just as soon leave him in a mess."

Marty shook her head, and begin washing the dishes in the washbasin. When she washed the first plate, she handed it to Tucker.

Tucker took it and turned the dish over in his hands. *What did she want done to it now? The thing was already as clean as a whistle. All this washing was a bunch of foolishness anyway.* Lots of times, Tucker had just wiped a handful of sand across a plate, knocked the dirt out and put it back in his pack. Opening the cupboard, Tucker started to put the dish away.

"Those need to be dried before you put them away," Marty told him.

Dry 'em? Shoot, they'd dry on their own. That's what Tucker thought, but he obediently picked up a rag, and took a couple of swipes across the face of the plate. Tossing it carelessly in the cupboard, he picked up the next dish.

"Where's your folks?" he asked. "I mean it's kinda strange for a young lady to be out here on her own."

Marty scrubbed a plate and eyed it critically before passing it to Tucker. "I don't know where they are. They left me with an uncle when I was young, I haven't seen them since."

Tucker didn't know what to say next, and wished he had never started this conversation. "You like living with your uncle?"

Marty smiled and her whole face lit up. "Oh yes," she said. "I mean, Uncle Jack was such a scamp, but I loved him dearly."

"What do you mean a scamp?" Tucker asked, more to keep the conversation going than to hear the answer.

"He ran a shell game on the docks. We moved around a lot, but Uncle Jack always made sure I had a roof over my head."

"Sounds like a nice guy, did he teach you to make up stories like the ones you've been telling us?"

"Yes, I guess he did," Marty admitted. "He always told me to trust no one."

"That's good enough advice, but kind of hard to follow. There comes a time when you have to trust somebody," Tucker replied, drying fast to keep up with her washing.

"Do you trust anyone?" Marty asked.

"Sure, I trust my men," Tucker answered uneasily.

Marty arched her eyebrows, showing her disbelief of that statement. "How about you? Do you have any family?"

"I have a half brother, we never got along, though," Tucker replied, drying the last dish and pitching it in the cabinet and slamming the door shut.

Marty watched Tucker walk over and sit beside the burly Weaver. At the mention of his family, Tucker's whole attitude changed. He said they didn't get along, maybe this was a sore subject. Reminding herself not to bring it up again, Marty wiped the tabletop dry and emptied the basin.

"You promised to tell us the story of the treasure," Weaver reminded, when Marty finished her cleaning.

"Okay," Marty agreed with a laugh. She pulled a chair to the center of the room. The men circled around her, eager to hear anything about the treasure. Just hearing about it made the treasure seem that much closer.

"Five years before Cortez arrived in Mexico and crushed Montezuma and the Aztecs, the Spanish sent out another ship. The diary my brother found was written by one of the ship's officers.

"According to the diary, their ship ran into heavy seas and wrecked off the coast of Mexico. After several days of wandering, they found a group of Aztecs fleeing from Montezuma's cruel reign. This group took the Spaniards in and welcomed them to the village."

"How'd they end up plumb up here in Colorado?" Tucker asked, impatient to get to the part about the treasure.

"They lived in the village for a couple of years, but then Montezuma found out about their village. He sent some warriors to destroy it and bring back the people to be sacrificed to the sun gods." Marty paused while the men lit up smokes.

"The villagers found out that Montezuma's men were coming and they packed up their belongings. That's when the Spaniards found out about the treasure. The villagers had raided Montezuma's temples before they fled his city.

"When they learned that Montezuma was coming for them, they fled north. Along the trail they encountered several bands of hostile savages. Finally they found the Black Canyon and settled there. The diary says they stayed there for a few years, until the savage tribes drove them out. They never had time to recover the treasure," Marty finished.

"What happened to them?" Weaver asked, fully stretched out on the floor.

"I don't know, they took off to the west. The diary peters out from there," Marty replied.

"Who cares about that?" Tucker demanded. "Break out that map and let's take a gander at it."

"I don't think so," Marty said, smiling sweetly. "It isn't that I don't trust you guys, but a girl can't be too careful. All you need to know is that we are going to a place called Black Canyon." Marty looked at the faces of the men, but she didn't notice that Hardy's face had turned chalk white. "You do know where that is, don't you?"

"Yes," Hardy answered simply. He clenched his fists to keep his hands from shaking. "I know of the place."

"Hot doggy, let's get going," Weaver said, fighting to set up.

Marty laughed, and reached out to pat his arm. "Go ahead and rest, I think we can wait until morning."

Before dawn the next morning they loaded their gear and set out. Before leaving, they shut Mason and Delbert in the root cellar. They left enough food and water for two weeks.

Tucker felt bad about leaving Delbert in the cellar, and said so to Weaver.

"Aw, don't worry about that boy, he'll be alright. His wound is healing nicely, and we'll be back in a week," Weaver assured.

Weaver's logic made sense, but Tucker still didn't like

it. As they moved through the trees, Tucker tried to settle in the saddle. His backside was healing, but remained tender.

Seeing Tucker's discomfort, Marty held out a pillow she had made from a red, checkered tablecloth. She'd even sewn some fringe around the edge of it.

Tucker eyed the pillow and shook his head. Disgustedly, he wrinkled up his nose, pushing the pillow away. He wasn't about to lug that thing around.

Marty laughed, tucking the pillow back in her saddle bag. "It's here if you change your mind," she said.

Tucker rolled his eyes, and spurred his horse to take the lead. Weaver and Hardy led the packhorses. One of them, a brown pony with a black mane, carried a full load of supplies and tools, appropriated from Mason's cabin.

Already, Danny and Weaver were arguing about something. Tucker sighed, riding with them two was worse than a bunch of kids. Still Tucker felt glad to see a little more life from Danny. The boy looked a lot better today. Color slowly returned to his cheeks and he talked of getting rid of the sling on his arm.

"You two want to bring everybody in the country down on us?" Tucker hissed, interrupting their spirited argument.

Tucker didn't worry too much about a posse, but as they rode deeper into the mountains the chance of meeting Utes increased. The Utes had been driven back into the mountains by the soldiers out of Fort Garland. As the San Luis Valley filled with farmers and ranchers, the Utes were forced deeper and deeper into the mountains.

Black Canyon lay in one of the last Ute strongholds. The route Tucker led them down passed right through the heart of Ute country. Tucker hoped they could slip in and out without being seen, but didn't much count on it. Nothing happened in this part of the country without the Utes knowing of it.

At noon, Tucker called a rest. "Should I cook something?" Marty asked, leading her horse up beside Tucker.

Tucker licked his lips and ran a finger along his jaw. "Alright, but I'll make the fire. We'll have to keep it small."

"Is there that much danger from the Indians?"

"You just bet there is. If they see us, it'll be fight or run depending on the situation."

"Couldn't you just talk with them? Explain that we mean them no harm?" Marty asked, opening the packs which contained the food.

"Maybe, I doubt it though. You never know about Indians, they are as fickle as all get out. They might decide to let us pass, and they might not," Tucker replied, putting the wood together for the fire.

"Weaver said this Black Canyon is a sacred place to them," Marty commented, waiting for Tucker to get the fire going.

"I heard that too," Danny said, squatting by the fire. He watched intently as Marty sliced bacon into a skillet over the fire.

Hardy and Weaver approached the fire after staking down all the horses. "You making some more of them biscuits?" Weaver asked, smacking his lips together.

"I haven't got the time, you'll just have to make do with the ones left from last night," Marty said, smacking the back of Danny's hand as he tried to sneak a piece of bacon from the skillet.

Grinning at their antics, Tucker raked up a pile of leaves and sat down. "Have you ever been to Black Canyon?" he asked Hardy.

"No, but I heard of it. The Utes have a legend that

whoever enters the canyon will never return alive and their spirits will be doomed to walk in the darkness forever."

"Aw horse hockey, I don't believe in any of that hogwash. Do you?" Weaver scoffed.

Hardy shrugged, watching the horses graze. "Those old ones had the knowing of a lot of things. They knew a lot that we can't understand," Hardy cautioned.

"They did know a lot we don't understand," Tucker agreed.

Weaver snorted loudly, snatching a biscuit from the sack Marty held. "You're not having second thoughts, are you?" he asked Tucker.

"Naw, if that gold's there, I mean to get it," Tucker answered. "I'm more afraid of the living Utes than any ghosts in a canyon."

After they had eaten, Tucker got everybody up and ready to move. Tightening his cinch, Tucker glanced around to make sure no one was watching him. Leading his horse, he sidled up to Marty. He helped her on her horse, and glanced around again.

"You still got that pillow?" he asked, looking at the ground.

"Sure," Marty replied, doing her best to look serious. "I thought you might be needing it," she added, digging it out of her bag.

Tucker looked at the tassels, and almost changed his mind. Where she got them, he had no idea. She must have been carrying them in her bag. Tucker felt certain she didn't find them at Mason's cabin.

Mounting the bay, Tucker slipped the pillow under his aching rear end. He caught Weaver watching him, and gave the big outlaw a severe look. Tucker jerked the lead rope roughly from the big outlaw. "You take the lead, I'll handle the packhorses for a while," Tucker ordered.

Tucker dropped back beside Hardy. "This is the Rio Grande we've been following?" he asked and Hardy nodded. "We won't be able to follow the river all the way?"

"No, soon the river will swing straight west. We must keep going northwest."

"That's what I thought." Tucker rubbed his jaw, looking ahead. "I've never been through this part of the country. Do you know the way?" Tucker asked, trying to recall everything he knew about these mountains.

"I've never been this way before. When I was with Marty's brother, we came out of Denver. We approached the canyon from another direction."

"I've heard of a pass through the mountains, then we'll come to another valley. From there it's a straight shot to the canyon. In the morning, I want you to ride ahead and find the pass."

"Are you afraid of the Utes?" Hardy asked. "They'll be watching the passes. They always do."

"I know," Tucker worried, rubbing his hands together. "But if we wander around the mountains looking for another way, they'll find us anyway. Mason is what concerns me now. He's liable to get loose and come looking for us."

Darkness came before they stopped for the night. Tucker helped water the horses, checking each animal carefully. He wanted the horses to be in good shape in case they had to make a run for it.

Assured that the horses were fine, Tucker hobbled to where the others gathered. Marty stopped digging through the packs to look at Tucker with a questioning look in her eyes.

"No fire," Tucker said, reading her look. "We'll need to keep a watch tonight."

Tucker gave the first watch to Danny. Tucker didn't expect trouble until morning, but he wasn't taking any chances. "Keep an eye on the horses. We can't afford to lose them," he told Danny.

Leaving the watch to the youngster, Tucker spread his bedroll. Accepting a piece of jerky from Marty, Tucker laid down on his stomach.

Chewing on the tough jerky, Tucker's eyes grew heavy. Every time he chewed, his eyelids dropped lower. The next thing he knew, Weaver was shaking him.

"Your turn for guard duty," Weaver said, fighting off a mighty yawn.

Tucker looked at the half-eaten piece of jerky in his hand. He started to toss it away, then shrugged and popped it in his mouth.

"Everything alright?" he asked, chewing slowly.

"Wind's blowing like a preacher man outside a cathouse, makes it hard to hear, but I ain't seen anything," Weaver replied, heading straight for his blankets.

Limping, Tucker circled the campsite. Like Weaver said, the wind was blowing hard. There was a kind of electricity in the air, and Tucker didn't care for the feel of the night.

He walked among the horses, petting them and talking softly. The horses were restless, tugging at their picket pins. Tucker continued to talk to them, rubbing their coats.

"Storm comes."

Tucker jumped at the sound of the voice. He spun around, drawing his pistol as he turned. His eased the hammer down, when he saw Hardy approaching. "I can see the stars," Tucker protested.

"The clouds are just over the mountains. They'll come pretty fast, I think," Hardy predicted, running his hands over the back of a gray pony.

Leaving Hardy to watch the horses, Tucker made a sweep around the camp. Swinging through the camp, he untied his long coat from the back of his saddle. Shrugging his shoulders into the coat, Tucker saw Marty huddled in a ball, trying to stay warm as she slept. For a moment, Tucker's face softened as he watched her. How lovely she looked in the moonlight!

On impulse, Tucker took his blanket and spread it over Marty. She moaned softly in her sleep, and pulled the blanket tight up around her shoulders. A gust of wind ruffled her hair. Tucker reached out a hand, touching her cheek lightly. He could feel the delicate softness of her skin.

Dropping his hand away from her face, Tucker rose and went to help Hardy with the horses. He didn't see the wistful smile playing on her lips as she rubbed her cheek where he touched it.

Tucker hurried to reach the horses. In only the last few minutes, the force of the wind had almost doubled. Even in the faint, silvery light of the moon, Tucker could see a dark mass of clouds rolling over the mountain tops.

In a matter of mere minutes, the stars disappeared and the night became pitch black. Now the wind shrieked through the trees, making hearing anything else impossible.

The wind sounded like the howling banshees of death Tucker had heard stories of when he was a kid. Shrugging off a shiver, not entirely caused by the wind, Tucker peered through the gloom.

Stumbling through the darkness, Tucker tried to reach the vague shapes of Hardy and the horses. Hardy had all the lead ropes in his hands. A couple of the horses spooked and tried to bolt.

Diving frantically, Tucker grabbed onto the ropes. The horses dragged both Tucker and Hardy a few yards. Gritting his teeth, Tucker dug in his heels and hauled back on the ropes.

Finally the horses stopped, their heads hanging and flanks

quivering. Working by feel, Tucker and Hardy strove to untangle the lead ropes.

A flash of lightning filled the entire sky with a blinding light. A horse screamed, and the smell of sulphur filled the heavy air.

Tucker heard Hardy curse as the first drops of rain fell. Small drops at first, the rain quickly built into a torrent. Working together, Hardy and Tucker pulled the horses inside the camp.

Weaver left the scanty protection of his poncho to help them with the mounts. Each horse had to be tied securely to a tree to keep them from bolting. Every few seconds, brilliant flashes of lightning lit the area. The lightning seemed to come from all around them. After each flash, Tucker could feel the hair on the back of his neck stand on end.

One of the horses Hardy held reared, his front hooves slashing through the air. Slipping in the mud, Hardy fell and lost his grip on the rope.

Tucker heard Hardy's cry, and saw the dark shape of the horse as the terrified animal bolted. Lunging through the darkness, Tucker grabbed the horse around the neck.

The pony slipped in the mud as Tucker's weight crashed into its neck. The horse fell heavily, throwing Tucker over its head.

Lying on his back, Tucker felt the lead rope slide across his stomach as the horse scrambled to its feet. Grabbing the rope, Tucker felt it tear through his hands, burning the skin off.

Lunging to his knees, Tucker used his hip to help hold the rope. The horse reared once, dragging Tucker across the muddy grass. Reaching up, Tucker got a short grip under the horse's jaw and brought the animal under control.

Trying to catch his breath, Tucker passed the rope twice around the trunk of a small tree, and tied it fast.

Collapsing against the tree, Tucker spit mud from his mouth, and sucked in deep gulps of the wet air. Climbing shakily to his feet, he called to Weaver and Hardy. His words were torn from his lips by the force of the wind. The lightning flashed, and he saw the pair looking about for him.

Tucker was surprised, in his battle to control the frightened horse, he'd been dragged a good forty feet. Lightning flashed again, and Tucker could hear a sizzle in the air.

The flash lit the clearing for a good five seconds. Tucker could see Marty huddled under a ground sheet. She looked from under one corner, motioning for Tucker to join her. Wasting no time, Tucker scooted under the sheet.

"How long will the storm last?" Marty asked, having to shout in Tucker's ear to be heard over the wind.

"I don't know. Not long I hope," Tucker shouted back, clutching a corner of the ground sheet with one hand and wiping water from his face with the other. The force of the wind made holding the ground sheet a battle.

For what seemed like hours, the storm raged on. But as the sun came up the wind backed off and the rain slacked into a cold drizzle. Wishing desperately for a cup of coffee, Tucker get everyone up and around.

Hardy saddled his horse and rode ahead, scouting for a pass. Tucker led the others, working his way through the mountains by feel. At times he could see a faint trail. A gray veil of cold rain kept visibility to a few yards.

Despite being cold, wet and thoroughly miserable, Tucker blessed the rain. Not only would the rain wash out their tracks, it would keep the Utes in their lodges.

They were a bedraggled bunch, when they stopped for lunch. Tucker kept a watch for Hardy as he munched on some jerky and a soggy biscuit.

Marty sat beside him, looking disdainfully at her meager meal. "What I wouldn't give for a hot meal and a cup of coffee," she complained, trying to brush her wet hair away from her face.

"What you might give is your life," Tucker answered bluntly. "Any fire today would give off a smoke column that could be seen for miles."

"I know that," Marty said irritably. "I was only wishing out loud."

"Eat fast, I want to cover as much ground as we can while the rain holds," Tucker instructed, rising to hustle the others up.

Marty stuck out her tongue and tossed her biscuit at his back. Popping the jerky in her mouth, she sucked the flavor from it.

She was using a piece of leather string cut from her saddle to tie her hair back, when Tucker gave the word to mount up. He stopped to boost her on her horse then led off.

"Least he could do is give a person a minute to rest," Marty complained to Weaver, as the big outlaw rode by. "I'm not used to riding like this. It seems like we've been going for days."

Weaver slowed his horse to let Marty catch up. "This ain't nothing," he allowed. "Why, I recall the time Long Jefferson was the sheriff in Wyoming Territory. One time he chased us for three solid weeks. I didn't think we'd ever give him the slip."

Marty looked at Weaver in disgust. What she wanted was a hot meal, not a lot of hot air. She could tell the big outlaw was just dying to tell her how they eluded the sheriff. Marty laughed at his eagerness. "Alright, I'll bite," she said. "How did you get away?"

Weaver's face brightened like sunlight on a new day. "Well now, ole Long he chased us so hard that he plumb tuckered himself out. One night, while he was sleeping, somebody slipped into his camp and spooked his horses.''

"That somebody wouldn't have been you?" Marty asked.

"Naw, I'm built too heavy footed for that. Tucker, he done it. We didn't wish Long dead, so we just run his horse off. While he spent a day catching his horse, we put some country behind us.''

"That's an interesting story, Mister Weaver, but it doesn't make me feel any less tired,'' Marty told him. The story didn't help her fatigue, but it did give her an idea.

Two hours later they caught up with Hardy. He sat on a rock, chewing on a piece of bark as they rode up. "I found a trail and a pass,'' he told them.

"The trail look well used?'' Tucker asked.

"I'd say so,'' Hardy replied.

"I don't like it one bit. Taking a well used trail in Indian country is a good way to lose your hair,'' Weaver declared.

"Did you see any signs of another trail?'' Tucker asked, and Hardy shook his head.

"Maybe there ain't no other trails,'' Danny suggested. "That might be why that trail is so well used, cause there just ain't no other way.''

"Whadda you know?'' Weaver scoffed, but then Danny's words sank in. "The boy might be right,'' he said slowly, hating to admit it.

Danny beamed, his eyes twinkling and a smile plastered across his face. Weaver saw the look and cuffed the youngster lightly. "Now don't go getting the big head. I said you might have a point. If it turns out you're right; it'll be the first time.''

Weaver's words had no visible effect on Danny. He still smiled, when he asked, "What are we gonna do?''

Tucker had already made up his mind. "Lead us to the

trail," he told Hardy. "If this rain holds, we should be alright."

"And if it doesn't?" Marty asked.

Tucker shrugged, showing his teeth in a flashing smile. "In that case, I guess we'll just have to trust in luck."

Hardy took the lead, in an hour he found the trail. They crossed a high pass and just before dark, they came on another pass. None of them particularly wanted to spend the night in the confines of a pass, so they pushed on.

After clearing the pass, the going was mostly downhill, so despite the dark, they made good time. When they finally stopped, everyone felt bone tired.

Nobody wanted to eat, and none of them talked. Except for Danny, who had first watch, they collapsed in their blankets.

Tucker had the last watch of the night. As the sun came up over the mountains, he woke his charges. The morning came bright and brilliant. The warmth of the sun made the cold and rain of yesterday seem a distant memory. A glowing confidence spread through the group, and they rode with new life.

Everyone except for Hardy. He rode with his usual emotionless expression, but his dark eyes were large and shifting about nervously. He no longer scouted ahead, riding with the pack instead. More and more, he showed an increasing reluctance to push ahead.

Unnoticed by the others, he took a small buckskin bag from his saddlebag and hung it around his neck. Tucked under his shirt, the bag was hidden from view, Hardy touched the bag often, reassuring himself that it was still there.

The bag had been made for him by his grandmother. She had been a full-blooded Cheyenne, and the bag contained magic. The bag possessed the power to ward off evil spirits.

Tucker led them down the mountain, and into a large valley. Not as large as the San Luis Valley, yet it was still magnificent. The trail skirted around the edge of the valley, so Tucker held to it. Rounding a shoulder of rock, which hung out of the trail, Tucker jerked his horse up short. The others, caught off guard by Tucker's sudden stop, crowded up behind him. "What the . . . ," Weaver started, then saw what caused Tucker to stop. A party of seven or eight Utes blocked the trail.

The surprise had been mutual. the Utes came to a ragged halt, staring hatefully at the white intruders. Then the lead warrior raised his lance.

Chapter Eleven

Irritably, Mason prowled the tiny root cellar. For the tenth time, he put his shoulder against the trap door and pushed. Whatever Tucker put on top of the trap was too heavy for Mason to move.

Perhaps, when Delbert got well enough to help, together they could push open the door. That would be a few more days at least, by then Tucker and his men would have the treasure and be out of the country.

Mason didn't believe for a second that Tucker would come back to free him and Delbert. Mason didn't believe, because if he were in Tucker's shoes, Mason wouldn't bother with coming back. Smacking his fist in his palm, Mason resumed his pacing.

Delbert sat on his bed, propping himself up with one elbow. The youngster watched Mason with interest. Lately, Mason had grown moody and irritable. Delbert feared that if Mason found a way out, he would leave Delbert.

"Can we get out?" Delbert asked, not sure he wanted out just yet.

"I don't know. I'm doing the best I can!" Mason snapped. Growling to himself, Mason stomped around the cellar. In a fit of anger, he swept a row of jars off the shelf.

As the jars shattered on the hard packed floor, Mason stopped, a sinister smile on his face. Reaching to the back of the shelf, Mason picked up a knife. He turned and held the knife up for Delbert to see. Delbert shrank back, not sure what Mason had in mind.

Mason stared at the knife lovingly. Rust had eaten away at the blade, and the handle was loose, but the knife looked beautiful to Mason.

Mason went to the outside wall, and buried the knife in the earth wall. Working quickly, he sawed out a fair sized chunk of dirt. Turning to Delbert, Mason smiled greedily. "Don't worry boy, we'll be out of here before long. Then we are gonna go settle a score with Tucker Evans and his bunch!"

Delbert swallowed hard, trying to screw up his nerve to ask the question which had been on his mind for days. "What's this treasure everybody's been talking about?"

Mason stopped digging to stare at young Delbert. "There's a fortune in old Spanish gold buried in the mountains. That girl has a map telling the exact location of the gold. If we want that gold we'll have to wipe out the whole bunch."

Delbert frowned, he didn't care for the sound of Mason's words. The thought of killing four men turned Delbert's stomach sour. "What about the girl?" he asked, his voice cracking.

Mason turned back to the wall, and resumed his digging. "You just forget about her. I'll take care of the young lady."

The lead warrior started to raise his spear, but stopped when Tucker smiled and held up his hands. For a long moment both sides stared at each other.

Holding the reins high and keeping his hands in sight, Tucker kneed his bay forward. Smiling and trying his best to look friendly, Tucker rode right up to the Utes. The lead brave spoke rapidly in harsh tones. He punctuated his words with sharp gestures.

Tucker glanced back at Hardy for an interpretation. "He wants to know why we dare to cross his land."

"Tell him, we go to the Black Canyon to pick up something sacred left there by our ancestors," Tucker instructed Hardy.

Hardy spoke rapidly to the Indians. When he finished, the Utes broke into an excited argument. Their leader silenced them with a savage sweep of his muscular arm. Once his braves were silent, the leader spoke to Hardy for a long time.

"He says that no one can enter the Black Canyon and return. The canyon will swallow them up. He says if we dare enter, our souls will be doomed to walk in the darkness of the canyon forever."

Tucker took his time, choosing his words with care. They just might get out of this without a fight. But he must be careful not to insult their beliefs. "Tell him our medicine is strong. We hope it will protect us. Tell him that we must honor our ancestors by getting the sacred stones left for us."

As Hardy delivered Tucker's message, the lead warrior stared at Tucker with growing respect in his eyes. When Hardy finished, the leader issued a barking order to his followers. Then he addressed Tucker.

He and Hardy exchanged a few sentences, then Hardy translated. "He says we must be very brave, and that he respects. He and his men will escort us to the canyon. They will wait outside the canyon for us. He didn't want Marty to go in with us, but I told him she is our medicine woman and she possesses great power."

"Why, thanks," Marty said cheerfully. "I think I like that."

The leader of the Utes spoke to his men, raised his lance aloft, and spun his pony around. As he led, his braves fell in around Tucker and his men.

Marty, watching the Utes carefully, steered her horse up close to Tucker's. "Do you trust them? How do we know they won't attack us later?" she asked, glancing over her shoulder.

"There's no way to know for sure, but I'd say they are on the level," Tucker answered. "Indians are curious folks. Maybe they just want to see if we'll have the guts to enter the canyon. The way they look at it, if we enter the canyon we're already dead so why waste energy killing us. Or maybe they didn't believe my story and want to see what we are really up to."

"Do they really believe all that nonsense about getting out of the canyon again?" she asked, still looking over her shoulder.

"You just bet they do," Tucker assured her. "If we don't go into the canyon, they'll despise us as cowards and probably just kill us on the spot."

"Do you believe it? The part about the canyon, I mean." Tucker grinned at her. "Naw, but they do and that's all that counts."

The Utes set a stiff pace which led them right to the mouth of the canyon in good time. Their leader stopped his horse well back from the canyon mouth. Turning his horse to face the whites, he made a lengthy speech.

"He says, they will camp here tonight. They will wait three days to see if we return. He doesn't think for a minute that we will be back," Hardy interpreted.

Tucker rode his horse up to the leader of the Utes. Looking the Indian squarely in the eye, Tucker extended his hand. Knowing this was the white man's symbol for respect, the Ute took Tucker's hand with a mixture of respect and disbelief in his dark eyes.

Holding Tucker's hand firmly, the Indian spoke. Hardy answered him quickly. "He said his name is Douglas, I told him your name,'' Hardy explained. ''I've heard of him, boss, he's a big man among them. Right hand man to Ouray, their big chief.''

''Douglas,'' Danny whispered as they rode away. ''I never heard of an Indian named Douglas before. I wonder how he got that name?''

''What do you care as long as they're being friendly?'' Weaver scoffed. ''If his name was Clarabell, he could still kill you just as dead.''

''I just wondered, that's all,'' Danny replied defensively.

''Likely some weak-hearted missionary gave it to him,'' Weaver decided. ''Now quit harping on that and let's go snag that gold!''

As he led his group into the canyon, Tucker turned and gave Douglas a salute. The Indians lined up watching respectfully as the whites entered the canyon.

Hardy held back, letting the others go first. Just before entering, Hardy stopped. As sweat rolled down his neck and chest, he grabbed the medicine bag hanging around his neck. He could hear the tom-toms of the ancient warriors pounding in his head. Drawing courage from his forefathers, Hardy clucked his horse forward. As soon as he entered the canyon, Hardy could feel the coolness.

Opening his eyes, he saw the others openly staring at him. ''Man, are you alright?'' Tucker asked, noting Hardy's chalky face.

Hardy forced a scowl on is his face and shouldered his horse past Tucker. ''Let's go get the gold,'' Hardy growled.

''That's right,'' Weaver agreed. ''Trot out that map and let's find the gold and get to spending it!''

Marty opened her purse, and reached inside. ''Keep your cotton picking fingers away from that cannon,'' Tucker warned loudly.

Marty gave him a superior look and pulled the map from

her purse. She unfolded it and studied the map, even though she knew every mark by heart. ''There's a sharp turn in the canyon about a mile in. Just past the bend is a stone marker. The treasure is buried directly across the canyon at the base of the south wall.'' As Marty finished, she passed the map to Tucker.

Tucker studied the map, then passed it back. ''Sounds simple enough. Let's go get the gold.''

Tucker lifted his reins and touched a spur to his horse. ''You coming, Hardy?'' he called, noticing Hardy hadn't moved. He simply stared at the canyon walls rising high above him. ''Hey! Hardy, let's shake a leg. I want to get the gold and get out of here as soon as we can.''

Hardy jumped in the saddle, tearing his eyes away from the canyon wall. Without a word, he started his horse. Kicking his horse into a trot, he caught up with the others. Suddenly, he wanted to stick close to the group.

Hardy could still hear the tom-toms beating in his ears. He wished he could paint his face in the tradition of his ancestors.

They might find the gold, but Hardy knew that none of them would ever leave the canyon again.

Chapter Twelve

Riding into the canyon, none of the others seemed overly concerned with the legend of the place. Weaver slouched in the saddle, enthusiastically explaining the finer points of spending money to young Danny.

"San Francisco, now that's the place we need to go," Weaver allowed. "They know how to treat a rich man there. The women are all pretty, and receptive to a man of wealth, if you know what I mean," Weaver added with a broad wink. Danny nodded eagerly, grinning, as he hung on every word.

"What do you know about San Francisco? When was you ever there?" Tucker asked from the head of the column.

"Well, I ain't never been there myself," Weaver admitted, "but I heard tell of the place. Once, I rode with a feller who spent the winter there. He told me all about the place." With that, Weaver launched into glorious stories of the grand lifestyle in San Francisco.

Tucker looked across at Marty, smiled and shook his head. He knew Weaver well enough to know the big outlaw was adding his own personal touch to each story. In most cases, Weaver was probably making the whole thing up.

"He sure makes it sound exciting," Marty commented with a laugh. "Perhaps we should go there."

For once, Tucker turned serious. "I'd like that, as long as we went together," he said softly.

Marty's eyes widened in surprise, then she looked away

quickly. "Let's go get the treasure first, then make plans," she said hastily.

Tucker didn't notice the quick change in her attitude. Like Weaver and Danny, Tucker was thinking about how he was going to spend the money. More and more, Marty began to creep into his thoughts. He stole a glance at her— perhaps the time had come to settle down.

Hardy didn't share the light mood enjoyed by the others. He rode almost standing in the stirrups, ready to leap from the saddle, or wheel his horse and make a break.

Several times, the urge to cut and run almost overpowered him. Once, he imagined he could hear the flapping of the leather wings of great bats. He knew the beasts wanted to feast on his flesh, leaving his soul to wander in the darkness, lost for all time. For an instant, Hardy's heart almost stopped, and his breath caught in his throat.

He couldn't see the bats, but he knew that was because they were phantoms. Perhaps they were only a warning. If they left now, maybe they could do so safely. Hardy's hand shook as he held the reins, his brain screaming for him to flee.

Tucker stopped, seeing the bend in the canyon ahead of him. He sat on his horse, savoring the moment. Dropping the reins, he vaulted lightly from the saddle. Tucker's nerves tingled as he walked around the bend.

The stone marker mentioned in the map stood against the north wall of the canyon. Kneeling down beside it, Tucker examined the marker.

The marker jutted up out of the canyon floor a good four feet. Tucker could see the marker had been laboriously chipped from a giant stone. Brushing away the dust, Tucker saw several lines of picture writing. Several strange words were mixed in with the pictures.

Intrigued by the marker, Tucker wanted to study it more,

but the fever to find the treasure gripped him. In long strides, he crossed the canyon floor. "Here it is!" he announced, stamping his foot on the spot.

"Let me at it!" Weaver shouted. Despite his bulk, Weaver leapt from the saddle. "I can already taste the wine in Frisco," he said, ripping one of Mason's shovels from the pack horse.

Weaver hurried to the spot where Tucker stood. The big outlaw dug with the fury of a man possessed, scattering dirt in every direction.

"I thought digging hurt your back," Danny called out cheerfully.

"You best be quiet, or I'll bolt your skinny behind to this shovel," Weaver threatened, the breath already whistling through his teeth.

After making sure that Weaver was digging in the right spot, Tucker went to fetch the other shovel. He saw that Hardy hadn't yet dismounted. The half-Indian stared at the rim of the canyon, with a faraway look in his eyes. The color had left his face, and he licked his lips continuously.

"What's the matter, Hardy? Did you see something?" Tucker asked, his eyes scanning the rim for a glimpse of what spooked Hardy.

Weaver stopped his digging to stare disgustedly at Hardy. "Don't tell me you put any faith in all that Indian foofaraw?" he scoffed.

Hardy nodded absently and dismounted. He took the shovel from an astonished Tucker, and walked like a man asleep to the spot where Weaver stood. With a last fearful look around, Hardy sank his shovel in the earth.

"Don't let it fret you none. When the time comes to leave, we'll get out of this hole if I have to knock one of the walls down," Weaver assured, giving Hardy a friendly pat on the shoulder. Weaver leaned on his shovel, looking up at the rim of the canyon. "Why just remember that time we was locked in that jail in Laramee. They claimed nobody could bust outta there. But we sure enough fooled them."

Weaver grinned at Marty. "Shoot, compared to gettin' out of that jail, leaving this canyon will be plumb easy. And if any of them spooks gets in our way, I'll twist their heads."

"How did you get out?" Marty asked, and Tucker snickered.

Ducking his head quickly, Weaver returned to his digging. "I don't rightly recall now. I suppose we used blasting powder or something," he mumbled.

"That ain't the way I remember it," Tucker corrected.

"How in the world do you expect a man to get any work done with all this jabberwalling going on? I swear a body can't even hear himself think," Weaver grumbled, digging hard and throwing dirt in every direction.

"What did happen?" Marty asked, smiling at Weaver's discomfort.

"Now let me see," Tucker said, dodging Weaver's shovel as the big man took a swipe at him. "As I recall, that widder woman who ran the boarding house sprang us."

Weaver grunted and kept at his digging. "Why did she do that?" Danny asked, laughing gleefully.

"We ain't got the time for all this conversation, we got a fortune to dig up," Weaver complained, ducking his head and giving all his attention to his digging.

Tucker ignored the big man. "The ol' gal had her sights set on hauling Weaver up in front of the preacher man. Course, she was off track in the head. She had musta been to be interested in a beat-up old fleabag like Weaver," Tucker answered, as Weaver's ears turned red. "Did you ever repay her kindness?"

"You gonna stand there gabbing all day, or help us dig?" Weaver demanded belligerently.

"While you men dig, I'll fix a nice supper," Marty offered. "That's if it's alright to have a fire," she added, looking questioningly at Tucker.

"Might as well. The Utes already know where we are at. No use hiding from them now," Tucker answered, moving over to relieve Weaver from his shovel.

Weaver gave up his shovel without much of a fight, and scrambled out of the already sizable hole. "You gonna make some more of them biscuits?" he asked, practically foaming at the mouth.

"Sure, maybe I'll make another pie."

"I could help," Weaver offered eagerly.

"That's alright, I can manage," Marty replied, laughing brightly. "You better help with the digging."

Weaver looked sourly at Tucker and Hardy as they worked. Bum arm and all, Danny waited restlessly for his turn at the shovel.

"Aw, alright, but I tell you, just a little dose of that shovel sure goes a long ways," Weaver griped.

Laughing, Marty pushed him away. Turning her back to them, she started a fire beside the stone marker. She was mixing dough for the pie, when she heard the shouts.

Abandoning her cooking, Marty rushed to the hole. The men were standing waist deep in the ground. They struggled to wrench a wooden chest from the bottom of the hole.

Using a shovel as a pry bar, Tucker lifted one end of the chest high enough for Weaver to get his hands underneath it.

Weaver turned red in the face as he stood the chest on one end. With Tucker and Hardy's help, he flopped it up on level ground. One side of the chest busted open, spilling the treasure out on the ground.

With a squeal of delight, Marty picked up a golden crown

with a shiny emerald in the center. "Isn't it beautiful?" she said, holding it up.

"It sure is," Weaver agreed. "You was right, there is a fortune here."

Tucker picked up a solid gold armband, judging the weight at almost a pound. "Danny, start sacking this stuff up. We'll dig up the other boxes," Tucker instructed, passing the armband to the youngster.

With a grin that extended clear across his face, Danny dug the gunny sacks out and started filling them.

"I'll finish supper. It'll be ready when you guys finish here," Marty said, a look of concentration on her face.

Instead of returning to the fire, Marty went to where she laid her clutch purse. She withdrew a brown bottle filled with white powder. Biting her lip, she looked from the bottle to the men working in the hole.

Her face hardened, and she strode to the fire. Hesitating for a heartbeat, she dumped the entire bottle in the dough for the pie crust. "I hope you knew what you were talking about, Uncle Jack," she whispered softly, as she stirred the powder in the dough.

Tucker and Hardy heaved the last box from the hole that was now almost six feet deep. Tucker boosted Hardy out of the hole. For a second, Hardy stared down at the hole they dug. "I don't like it, it looks like a grave," Hardy said. Shaking his head, he extended a hand down, pulling Tucker out of the hole.

Danny and Weaver already had the chest cracked open, and were busy sacking the stuff up. They had found crowns, necklaces, armbands and even bowls made from pure gold.

Tucker didn't have any idea how much the stuff would be worth, but he felt sure it was over a million dollars. Never very good at arithmetic, Tucker tried to figure out how many horses a million dollars would buy. Not even in his wildest dreams could Tucker imagine this much money.

"Man, there's enough gold here to buy San Francisco," Weaver declared, tying the top on the last sack.

"Is that the last of it?" Marty called from the fire. She kept up with their progress by listening to their talk.

"That's the end of it. Is supper ready?" Tucker asked.

"The food's been ready for a few minutes, I was just waiting for you guys to finish up," Marty replied.

"Let me at it!" Weaver shouted. "All this work sure made me hungry."

When they reached the fire, Marty already had their plates dished up. She placed a hunk of pie on each of their plates.

"You're not having any pie?" Tucker asked.

Marty turned her back, dishing up her own food, a single tear rolling down her cheek. "No, you guys did the work. You eat the pie." she answered softly.

Chapter Thirteen

A wave of relief swept over her as Marty left the absolute darkness of the canyon. The canyon seemed to have a personality of its own. It exuded a dark brooding quality, almost an evil aura.

Turning for a last look, Marty took her first easy, deep breath since entering the place. Looking back reminded her of what she had done. She hated herself for drugging Tucker and his friends.

Did she do right?

Marty told herself over and over that she did the only thing she could have done. A woman alone couldn't trust anyone. A woman alone with a fortune in gold and diamonds surely couldn't afford to trust anyone.

Marty recalled what her uncle had told her; where money or a woman was involved, no man could be trusted. Her uncle had drilled that into her over and over.

A wistful smile came to her troubled face as Marty thought of her late uncle. She knew he had been a scamp, probably worse. But all her heart remembered was a kindly, sweet man.

Unconsciously, Marty compared her uncle and Tucker. They would have liked and understood each other. They were so much alike, just a little too restless to fit in.

Marty hated to think that Tucker might have taken the treasure from her, but if he and his men wanted to, they could've done that very thing.

Misty-eyed and with a lump in her throat, Marty turned her horse and started south. Right away, she found out that handling a string of packhorses was going to be a job. In the canyon, the horses had been content to follow. Now in the openness of the valley, they tried to pull away.

Marty had too many lead ropes to wrap them all around the saddlehorn. She didn't know how to string them all together as the men had done.

Concerned with the horses, Marty didn't see the Indians until she bumped into them. She gasped and tried to run, but a tall Indian grabbed her reins and held them fast.

Peering intently through the gloom of the night, Marty finally recognized the Indian as Douglas, the leader of the bunch that led them to the canyon.

The Indian spoke in rapid tones. His manner seemed agitated as he spoke again, gesturing to the mouth of the dark canyon.

Through a series of gestures, Marty explained to him that the canyon had swallowed them up. The Indian shook his head, motioning for Marty to be silent.

He turned to one of his men and spoke in harsh tones. One of the bunch broke off and raced away to the west. The leader dropped Marty's reins. For a wonderful second, Marty thought they were going to let her pass, but then the Indian crossed his arms across his chest. He sat on his horse, blocking Marty's path, an intense look on his dark face.

Tucker woke slowly, his head buzzing and his eyes not quite in focus. Groggily he sat up, rubbing his aching head. His tongue felt thick and fuzzy as he looked about for a canteen.

Spying the coffee pot by the dead fire, Tucker rolled over and picked up the pot. He tossed the lid away and drank right from the pot. The cold coffee tasted only slightly better than the fuzz in his mouth.

Raising the pot to his lips for another drink, Tucker's eyes fell on the empty picket line. Spitting the coffee out, he tossed the pot over his shoulder.

Weaver was just setting up, trying to shake off the effects of the heavy sleep, when the flying coffee pot hit him in the forehead. Groaning, the big outlaw collapsed back in his blankets.

Ignoring Weaver, Tucker let out a howl and bounded to his feet. Stumbling and slipping, Tucker ran over to where the horses had been tied. Every horse in the string was gone!

Forcing his bloodshot eyes to focus, Tucker scanned the ground for tracks. Right away, he spotted where the heavy packs had been drug along the ground.

Cursing mightily, Tucker ran to wake the others. He tripped over a saddle and fell sprawling across Danny. "Wake up, kid," Tucker shouted, shaking Danny.

Weaver tried sitting back up. Already he had a lump over his eye. "Who hit me?" he wanted to know.

"Never mind that, just wake up Hardy," Tucker growled. As he went to wake Marty, Tucker wondered how Mason had gotten loose so fast. Stopping dead in his tracks, Tucker realized her bed was gone.

"She's gone!" Tucker grabbed a saddle and flung it across the camp. "That conniving female took our gold and left us here afoot!"

"How did she manage to load the packs and sneak out of camp without waking us?" Weaver asked.

Hardy sat up slowly, his dark face sagging. "Something in the food," he answered. "A powder in the food to make us sleep a long time."

Hardy climbed stiffly to his feet, immediately casting

about for tracks. "She didn't take our riding horses, they went up the canyon," he decided after a brief inspection.

A few minutes later, four very angry men set out walking up the canyon. None of them enjoyed walking, but Weaver suffered more than the others. The big outlaw complained fiercely at the necessity for walking.

"I can't hardly believe she'd do us this way. I sorta liked that girl," Weaver complained, shaking his head sadly.

Tucker walked in silence, his mood swinging back and forth. First, he felt furious with Marty, plotting all sorts of revenge against her. The next minute, he found himself remembering the night they spent huddled under the blanket.

He could vividly recall the sweet way she smelled, and the warmth of her body pressed up against his. Then his anger returned, he cursed himself for thinking such treacherous thoughts. Imagine he, Tucker Evans, being sucked in by a pretty face. Oh, but what a face!

Kicking sand and feeling thoroughly miserable, Tucker trudged along, trusting the others to follow the trail of the missing horses.

After three and a half hours of walking, they found Weaver's sorrel. Tucker caught the sorrel by the ear, and slipped the bridle on. "I'll take this horse and go after Marty," Tucker stated flatly.

"Whoa, hold on a minute," Weaver protested. "We need this horse to catch the others."

"I said, I'm taking this horse," Tucker repeated slowly, his eyes staring defiantly. "Do any of you have any objections?"

Hardy shrugged and sat down on a rock. Danny started to protest, then looked to Weaver for support. The big outlaw shook his head. When Tucker got his temper up, there was no reasoning with him.

Tucker's face softened, and for a minute, he returned to

his old smiling self. "When I catch up with Miss Martha Flynn, I'll take the treasure and meet you in Santa Fe."

With that, Tucker vaulted onto the sorrel. He rode the horse hard back to camp. Sliding the sorrel to a halt, Tucker ran to his saddle. Gathering up the saddle and blanket, Tucker glanced around the camp for anything he might need. Seeing nothing he wanted, Tucker saddled the sorrel and took off.

He figured Marty had at least eight hours start on him. Eight hours, unless she stopped during the night. As he thought about it, Tucker decided the chances were good that she did stop sometime during the night. After all, Marty did not know the country, and she had little experience in traveling across rough country. Marty was a smart girl, she wouldn't take a chance on getting lost at night.

Cheered, Tucker felt sure he would catch her by nightfall. When he caught her, Tucker vowed he would teach that young lady some manners.

Mason cursed as the tunnel caved in on him. Spitting dirt, he backed out of the hole, trying to shake the dirt from his hair. "Another cave in?" Delbert asked from his blanket.

Mason ignored Delbert's question, since it was perfectly obvious that the tunnel had caved in. Reaching in to the hole, Mason scooped the loose dirt out, piling it on the floor. Each time he drug an armload out, more dirt cascaded down. Putting a rein on his temper, Mason stuck doggedly to his job. Soon, he could see a shaft of light from the top of the hole. Taking the knife, he jabbed viciously at the ceiling of his hole.

Dirt showered over his head and shoulders, but in minutes he had the hole at the top of his tunnel big enough to stick his head through.

Squirming in the hole, Mason pushed his head through the hole. A breeze cooled the sweat on his face. The sunlight seemed bright after days in the cellar.

Turning his shoulders, he pushed one arm through the opening. He tried to lever himself up and out with one hand, but the earth kept caving off around him. He could feel the dirt building up around his knees, soon he would be trapped.

Moving carefully, he leaned out and caught the corner of his house with his free hand. Pulling against the rough logs Mason managed to work his other hand up and out of the hole. Once both shoulders were above ground, he pulled himself out easily.

Flopping over the edge, Mason lay on the ground, breathing like he had just run a mile. He could hear Delbert calling from the cellar.

Ignoring Delbert, Mason climbed shakily to his feet. Holding on to the corner of the cabin, he bent over, trying to catch his breath.

His breathing more stable, Mason crossed around to the front of the house. He considered leaving Delbert in the cellar. The boy'd proved to be a bigger pain than a help.

Mason could still hear Delbert yelling, a desperate tone in his wailings now. Scowling, Mason kicked the front door of the cabin open. Picking up the feed sacks Tucker had piled on top of the trap door, Mason tossed them aside. With each sack, he put more force in the toss. The last one flew halfway across the room, breaking a chair when it landed.

"You still down there, boy?" Mason called through the trap door. Even in the bad light, Mason could see the relief wash over the boy's face.

"I thought you was gonna leave me," Delbert said weakly.

Mason didn't respond, instead he got to his feet and

crossed to the bunk beds. He jerked the mattress off the bottom one. Under the mattress was a gun and holster belt.

Mason pulled the pistol from the holster and checked the loads. Assured that the gun was loaded, Mason draped the belt over his shoulder, ramming the pistol down in his pants.

He crossed the floor to the cellar opening. Poking his head down in the trap door, he hollered at Delbert, "I've got some horses in a corral back up the canyon. I'm going to go get them."

"Could you at least help me up out of this hole first?" Delbert asked, almost pleading.

Mason didn't answer. As Delbert listened to the hollow sound of Mason's boots on the floor, he knew Mason didn't intend to come back.

Chapter Fourteen

Marty followed behind the Indians. She didn't feel at all comfortable, but at least now they had someone who could speak English. He was a small brave, who continually squinted as if he needed glasses.

"Chief Douglas wants to know what happened to the men," he said, dropping back beside Marty.

Marty had been thinking about her story all night. "They were destroyed in the canyon. A terrible wind came up, tearing the skin and flesh from their bodies. In minutes, all that was left was bones."

The small Ute nodded and looked at Marty with respect. "Douglas said this would happen. He told me you are a medicine woman. You must possess great power to have survived."

He left Marty, riding ahead to relay her words to his chief. The Indians talked wildly among themselves. They gestured at Marty, moving away, giving her plenty of space.

The small brave dropped back beside Marty. "You have a place of honor among these warriors. They will tell the story of the powerful medicine woman who went into the dark canyon and returned. They will tell their children of your legend."

"I'm flattered," Marty said, and decided that she rather liked the idea of being a legend. As long as the Utes believed she was a medicine woman, she figured she would be safe.

"I'm just sorry that I could do nothing for the men in my party."

The small warrior shrugged, unconcerned with that. "They were non-believers. Nothing could save them."

Marty didn't reply, feeling sad all at once. Tucker's men had believed. They had believed in her anyway, that's why they hadn't returned from the canyon.

The small Ute saw the sadness in her face. He thought she mourned for her friends lost in the canyon. He kept silent, respecting her grief.

Truth was, Marty felt bad about the thing she had done. She wasn't proud about the story she spun to the Utes, but that was the least of it. Marty felt a burning shame about leaving Tucker's men sitting in the canyon with nothing.

Marty glanced back at the pack horses carrying the bulging sacks of treasure. She should have left some of it for Tucker and his men. At least one sack. At the time she hadn't thought of it, eager only to get away.

Closing her eyes, Marty could hear Weaver's booming laugh and continuous stories. She could see Hardy's rare smiles and Danny's eagerness to be accepted as one of the group.

Mostly, she saw Tucker. His ever-smiling face. She remembered his energy and drive. She felt choked as she recalled the first time she ever saw him.

He'd presented a breathtaking sight, charging down that rocky slope toward the stage, a reckless smile on his face. Shaking her head to rid herself of the memories, she rode in miserable silence.

The Utes rode at a steady pace all day. Late in the afternoon a brave who had been riding far in the lead rode back to meet them.

Marty's interpreter explained the conversation. "The

scout has sighted a party of white men. They are your people?''

"I don't know," Marty said, trying to decide if she wanted to meet a bunch of white men or not.

Douglas spoke quickly and decisively. "He says we will take you to the white wagon train. They are your people, and they will see that you get to where you are going in safety," the small brave interpreted.

They crossed a small stream and topped a saw-toothed ridge. Down in a small glade, Marty could see ten or twelve wagons.

As the Utes stopped, each man shook hands with Marty, showing their respect for her. The small warrior handed Marty the lead rope for the pack animals. Then, in seconds, they vanished into the forest, as if they had never been there at all.

Marty tied the lead rope around her saddlehorn. The Utes had strung the animals together, making them much easier for Marty to handle.

As Marty descended the ridge, she could see several people working around the wagons. Most stopped what they were doing to stare at her. Marty's mind raced as she tried to come up with a story to tell them. They would be surprised to see a woman alone in this part of the country. Likely, they would wonder what she had in her packs.

A tall rangy man with dark curly hair and a red tinted beard stepped to the front. "Good day to you, Missy," he said politely. The man's eyes took in Marty and her heavily loaded pack horses. "Looks like you have quite a load there."

Marty gave him a flashing smile, wishing she had taken the time to comb her hair and brush her clothes. "I do have a heavy load, and my horses are tired. I was hoping I could make a trade for fresh ones."

The leader pulled at his beard thoughtfully. "We might be of a mind to make a deal. We were just fixing to have coffee, come to the fire and we'll discuss it."

Marty wanted to be going. She knew Tucker would be following, and she didn't care to face his anger. Still, coffee would taste good. Maybe she could get something to eat. It had been so long since Marty had eaten she had almost forgotten what it was like.

"Why thank you, sir. I believe I will accept your hospitality. However, I can't stay long, I'm running late as it is."

The man gave Marty a quizzical look, wondering where she could be going and why she was late. "Hobart, take care of the lady's horses," he said, snapping his fingers at a gangling boy. "My name is Jacob McGilvey, this is my wife Estelle. The boy, Hobart, is my son."

"I'm Martha Flynn," Marty said, handing her reins to Hobart.

McGilvey mumbled something about being pleased to make her acquaintance as he led Marty inside the circle of wagons. Several fires burned inside the circle. Marty could see the women going about the business of preparing the evening meal. A pack of rambunctious youngsters dashed back and forth between the wagons.

"So you wanna trade for fresh animals?" McGilvey commented, handing Marty a cup of coffee.

"Yes, sir," Marty replied. "Do you think that would be possible?"

Jacob McGilvey pondered the question for a moment, then shrugged. "Who knows. I'll ask among the men, see if any of them is interested in making a swap," he replied, sounding doubtful. He left Marty, and walked to where a group of men worked on a busted wagon wheel.

"Here, dear, I thought you must be hungry," Estelle McGilvey said, extending a bowl and spoon to Marty.

Marty thanked her politely, taking the bowl from the older lady. Glancing in the bowl, Marty saw it contained a mush of cornbread and beans. The meal didn't look very appealing, but Marty was hungry and decided this wasn't the time to be finicky.

Tasting the food cautiously, Marty found that it tasted far better than it looked. Eating quickly, she finished the bowl and emptied her coffee cup. Marty would have liked another bowl, but decided it wouldn't be polite to ask for more.

McGilvey came back with two men. "These men are willing to make a swap, but they'd need some money on top," McGilvey said, sounding apologetic.

"How much?" Marty asked, eyeing the two men warily.

A short, broad man in a sweat-stained shirt explained. "Well, the riding horse is a fine animal. Three of the pack horses are certainly good enough, but the pinto—he ain't much. Besides, the animals sure are tuckered out, it'd be a couple of days before we could work them."

"How much money do you want?" Marty repeated firmly.

The two men exchanged looks. "Eighty dollars," the short man said finally.

"Eighty dollars! I don't have that kind of money," Marty exclaimed.

The two would-be traders looked sad and shrugged their shoulders. The taller man spoke for the first time. "We'd like to help you out, Missy, but that's the best we can do," he said, sounding sorry. "My advice to you is to spend the night with us. You can use your horses tomorrow if you take it slow and easy."

"I can't do that," Marty replied quickly, alarmed at the

prospect. "I must be going soon." Marty stopped, seeing the confused looks on the men's faces. "My two sons are home alone, I need to get home tonight. The oldest is only fourteen."

"You don't hardly look old enough to have a fourteen year old son," Estelle McGilvey said, looking at Marty closely.

"They're actually my stepsons, but I still worry about them being home alone," Marty added hastily.

"How far is it to your home?" Jacob McGilvey asked, pulling at his beard again.

"Ten, twelve miles," Marty answered, wondering if that was too far or too close. "My husband is coming along behind me. He should be along tonight or early in the morning. He could pay you the money for the horses," Marty suggested.

The two men making the trade shook their heads, starting to protest. Jacob McGilvey silenced them with a sweep of his hand. "Alright, Mrs. Flynn, we'll make your trade," Jacob said.

"Hold up a minute, Jacob, I ain't gonna make the trade unless I get my money up front," the short, broad man protested.

"Be quiet, Luke," McGilvey said. "I was elected captain of this train to make such decisions. I've made up my mind and that's final. We'll do the Christian thing and help the young lady."

McGilvey instructed his son to change Marty's saddle and the packs to the fresh horses. Marty fidgeted impatiently, while the boy worked.

Suppose he or one or the men helping him busted open one of the packs? Marty cringed every time they picked up one of the sacks, but after what seemed like hours, they had the stuff switched and Marty was ready to go.

Marty thanked McGilvey sincerely and shook his hand before she mounted and rode away.

McGilvey watched Marty ride away, wondering how much of her story he could believe. "I don't like it, Jacob, I don't think we will ever see that eighty dollars. I doubt if her husband will show," the short, broad Luke complained bitterly.

"Somebody will come. I am sure of that," McGilvey said calmly.

"You believed her then?" Luke demanded.

"Not entirely, but she was in a fearful hurry. I'd say someone or something is chasing her. I'd be willing to bet that a man shows up here in the morning looking for her."

"Well, all I got to say is, he'd better have eighty dollars," Luke allowed, belligerently. "Cause if he don't, I'm gonna take it out of his hide!"

Chapter Fifteen

Deke Carlin stopped at the mouth of the canyon, which led up to Mason's cabin. He could see the tracks going in, and the ones coming back out. He knew Tucker wasn't in the canyon, but his curiosity made him go check it out.

Anyway, a few more hours wouldn't matter. He was already so far behind Tucker that catching up would be next to impossible.

Deke rode into the yard, his horse's hooves clopping on the hard-packed yard. The cabin door hung open, and the place looked to be deserted. Deke peeked inside the cabin, and seeing no one, started to leave.

As Deke turned to go, a weak voice called from inside the cabin. Dismounting, Deke drew his pistol and crept inside. The voice called again, as Deke crossed the room to the open trap door.

Looking in the cellar, Deke saw a young man lying on a pile of blankets. "What are you doing down there, son?"

"I was locked down here. My leg is hurt, and I can't get out by myself," Delbert answered, his voice hoarse from shouting.

"Who locked you down here?" Deke asked, dropping down in the cellar.

"A bunch of outlaws. They shut me and a man named Mason down here. Mason got out, but he ran off and left me."

"These outlaws, were they the Tucker Evans gang?"

118

Deke asked, and Delbert nodded. "Did they have a young lady with them?"

"Yeah, I liked her. She helped fix my leg up," Delbert replied.

Deke's face turned red, and he swore. "What's the matter, mister?" Delbert asked.

"That dang fool Tucker. He went and robbed the bank in Del Norte, and with Miss Flynn along. He was supposed to help her rescue her brother from the Utes," Deke said bitterly. "I should have known better than to let her leave with him."

"They didn't rob the bank in Del Norte," Delbert said, firmly. "I thought they did at first, but I heard them talking. They were upset about the bank being robbed. Besides, they didn't have any money."

"Are you sure?" Deke demanded fiercely.

"I'm sure. They was worried about getting enough money to outfit a trip into the mountains."

"Then they went after Marty's brother?" Deke asked, starting to feel better.

Delbert shook his head slowly. "I don't know anything about that," he said. "The lady had a treasure map. They went into the mountains to get the treasure."

A puzzled look crossed Deke's face, replaced quickly by a flash of understanding. Slapping his thigh, he threw back his head and laughed. Marty had conned them all. A twinkle in his eye, Deke shook his head. Tucker better watch out, there was more to the young lady than met the eye. To think that Deke had been worried about her, she'd probably end up dealing Tucker out of his share of the treasure.

Still chuckling, Deke leaned back down to the trap door. "I'll get you upstairs," Deke told Delbert. "Tomorrow, I'll take you home."

"No, sir," Delbert replied, shaking his head. "There's something I got to do first."

"What's that, son?" Deke asked. "You should be home resting."

Delbert folded his arms across his chest, his young face looking grimly determined. "That man Mason I told you about. He's going after them. He wants the treasure. He's gonna kill Tucker and his men, and take Miss Flynn away. I gotta stop him!"

Hardy, Weaver and Danny sat back at their original camp inside the canyon. They found two of the horses, but the third eluded them.

"What do you think, Hardy? Should we try and find the other horse, or drag outta here on two?" Weaver asked.

Hardy shrugged, chewing on a piece of jerky. "It does not matter. We will never escape this place."

"Are you still harping on all that hocus pocus? I swear, you're gettin' worse than a Sunday school teacher. I don't know what's got into you. You didn't used to be scared of nothing," Weaver said in exasperation.

Hardy sat in silence, slowly chewing his food without really tasting it. He felt sure they would die when they tried to leave the canyon. One extra horse wasn't going to change that.

"If you were paying more attention to things, we might have found the other horse. You're supposed to be the tracker of this outfit," Weaver pointed out. "Tucker and Marty both left, and tomorrow so will we."

Hardy shook his head sadly. "No, they did not make it. Last night in my dreams, I heard their souls crying from the darkness."

"Aw phooey, the only thing you heard crying last night

was my tired aching feet,'' Weaver said, waving his hands at the despondent Hardy.

Young Danny looked at both of them, licking his lips. ''I don't know, Weaver, maybe we should leave tonight.''

''Don't tell me you are starting to believe all those old spook tales too. This is as good a place to camp as we'll find. First thing in the morning we'll leave. Maybe when we get out of this Godforsaken hole in the ground, the two of you will get your senses back.''

Tucker glanced at the setting sun, fuming as he worked the trail out. He hadn't counted on Marty teaming up with the Utes. They were leaving the country at a pretty good clip. Tucker managed to close the gap some, but still remained several hours behind.

Looking to the sky, Tucker cursed bitterly. Already the sun was sinking low. When darkness came, he would have to stop. He couldn't chance losing the trail.

Darkness caught Tucker before he found a good place to camp. Too tired to care, he simply pulled back in some trees, tended to his horse, and spread out his blankets.

The ground sloped away and proved to be rocky, but Tucker was tired enough that it didn't matter. In minutes after lying down, he fell asleep.

He woke before daylight, fixed himself a meager breakfast, and was in the saddle by first light. An hour later, he topped the ridge and spied the wagon train. He noted that the Utes had left Marty, their tracks leading away to the west.

''Got you!'' Tucker said grimly. He felt sure Marty would be with the wagon train. Jerking his hat lower, he started down the rocky slope, intending to give that girl a piece of his mind when he found her.

As Tucker started off the ridge, Jacob McGilvey spotted

him. Jacob studied the man closely. All morning, Jacob had stared up at the slope, waiting for the rider he knew would come. It didn't surprise him that the rider looked exactly like Marty's description of her husband.

"You looking for a young lady with a passel of pack animals?" McGilvey asked, as Tucker approached.

"That's right. Is she here?"

"She came by yesterday evening, traded for fresh critters, then took off like a scalded dog," Jacob McGilvey answered, and Tucker swore quickly. "She owes eighty dollars for the horses. She allowed as how you'd pay."

"That ain't likely," Tucker replied grimly.

"Ain't you her husband?" Jacob asked.

Tucker snorted loudly. "No, not hardly," Tucker assured. "And I ain't paying no eighty dollars either."

Before McGilvey could respond, Luke Sherrier stalked up, his face dark with anger. "The lady said you would pay. She even described you to a tee. She said you was her husband," Luke said, through clenched teeth. "Now, you gonna pay or not?"

Tucker smiled daringly. He folded his hands on the pommel of the saddle, and leaned back. "If she took you for eighty dollars, that just proves you are as dumb as you look, and if you think I'm gonna pay you anything, then, brother, you are stupid."

For just a second Luke looked confused, thrown off by Tucker's smile and soft tone. Then his mouth fell open in shock. Anger quickly replaced the shock. His face turned so red, Tucker thought he would explode.

Luke started to hurl back an angry reply, but something in the stranger's taunting smile brought him up short. Instead of blustering, he turned to the circle of wagons, waving his arm above his head.

Five rifle barrels poked out from underneath the canvas tops of the wagons. Tucker's smile didn't fade, nor did his expression even flicker, but inside he tightened like a spring.

Tucker didn't have the eighty dollars. He didn't have eighty cents!

"Are you ready to pay now?" Luke Sherrier asked, placing his hands on his hips.

Tucker leaned forward in the saddle, the taunting smile still plastered on his lips. "Eighty dollars isn't much to die for," he said softly. "I don't know what story she told you, but the truth is she stole those packs and horses from me."

"That may be true, and it may not, but it makes no never mind. We're still out eighty bucks," Sherrier maintained.

Tucker shrugged, straightening up in the saddle. "It's up to you friend. Whether you live or die, it's all up to you."

Luke Sherrier didn't budge an inch. He folded his hands across his chest, every line of his body screaming with stubbornness.

"The way I see it is even if them was your horses like you claimed, you still owe the money. We made a fair deal, so when you pay us, then you can go find your stuff and everything will be even."

Luke looked at Tucker, waiting for a response. All he got was the same daring smile. "You owe the money, mister, and by all that's holy, you're gonna pay! Ain't that right men?" Luke growled threateningly.

A chorus of yes sirs, and you bets rang out from inside the circle of wagons.

Jacob McGilvey felt sick inside. He turned his back, and stared at the distant peaks, washing his hands of the whole deal. He never thought things would progress this far. At least one man, and maybe more was going to die for eighty dollars!

McGilvey let this happen simply because he wanted to see who was following Martha Flynn. McGilvey never dreamed that the man wouldn't pay the eighty bucks. Now if he didn't, this man was going to die!

Chapter Sixteen

Marty awoke with a start, knowing she overslept. Sleep hadn't come easy last night. She had heard a threat in every sound, her imagination dreaming up all sorts of horrors in the looming shadows of the forest.

Rolling her bedroll, Marty dearly wished for a cup of coffee and something hot to eat. She couldn't afford to take the time, nor risk building a fire. The smoke could be seen for a long way on a clear morning. Tucker told her that.

Tucker. She wished she could keep him out of her mind. Every time she turned around, he snuck into her thoughts.

After gathering her gear, Marty saddled her horse, and looked at the packs in dismay. The very thought of loading them filled her with discouragement. They were so heavy. It required every ounce of her strength to lift even one of the bags.

Knowing she was stalling, and that she needed to be moving, Marty started to work. She hoisted the pack saddles onto the horses, then one by one she lifted the bulging sacks, hooking them on the saddles. She resisted the impulse to open one of the sacks and gaze at the lovely treasures inside.

An hour passed before she managed to heave all the sacks into place and lash them down. Tired from the exertion, Marty wanted to rest a few minutes before starting, but didn't dare.

She held little faith in her trick at the wagon train to hold Tucker for long. Knowing Tucker the way she did, Marty didn't think it would take him long to worm out of that one. It never even occurred to her that Tucker might have to kill a man to get away, or be killed trying.

Despite everything she had seen since coming west, Marty never dreamed a man could be killed over a mere eighty dollars.

Wiping the perspiration from her brow, Marty mounted her horse. Taking her bearings from the sun, she set out in a southwesterly direction. Riding slowly, she tried to remember everything she had heard about this country.

The way she figured it, the state line had to be close. Once over the line, Santa Fe wasn't too far. Marty felt confident that she could find the place. Getting into town worried her, though.

Everyone in town would be curious about her packs. If they even suspected what the packs contained, Marty felt sure the treasure would be taken from her.

Suddenly, she thought of Deke Carlin. He had been riding the stage bound for Santa Fe. Perhaps she should enlist his help. Deke had seemed to like her. One thing was for sure, nobody would try anything with Deke around.

Marty shook her head. She couldn't trust anyone, not if she wanted to keep her treasure. And Marty wanted to keep it. These packs represented everything she had in the world. Without the treasure, Marty didn't know what she'd do. Not many jobs were open to women, almost none that were considered proper.

No, this was a problem she must handle by herself. If she just put her mind to it, Marty told herself, she could find a way to get the gold into town. Once it was safely deposited, she could relax.

She tried to imagine what Tucker might have done. She knew he would have come up with a creative solution.

Irritated with herself, Marty re-checked her course, studying the trail behind her. She half expected to see Tucker and his men riding up behind her. The trail, however, remained empty, and Marty felt alone.

Being alone bothered her. She wanted to push on faster, but forced herself to keep the pace slow. She wanted her horses fresh in case trouble arose. There was no reason to run, not until she saw something to run from.

The mountains ended abruptly. In one breathtaking instant, she rounded the shoulder of a mountain and the sky opened up before her. She jerked her horse to a stop as the trail disappeared over an impossible looking cliff.

She dismounted, tied her horse to a tree, and crept up to the edge. A chill raced up and down her spine at the sight of the trail—it dropped away almost six hundred feet.

Marty could see a couple of switchbacks, but even so, the path looked impossibly steep. From her altitude, the trail looked no wider than a ribbon.

Her legs shaking, she went back to her horse. She started to lead him, but then changed her mind. She trusted her horse's balance on the steep trail more than her own.

Her horse shied back from the dropoff, not liking the looks of that trail one bit. But after some coaxing from Marty, he started down. The horse locked his front legs, half walking and half sliding down the steep path.

The ride was rough, and now Marty wished she had walked. It was too late now, all she could do was point her feet forward, lean back in the saddle and hang on.

The lead rope tied to her saddle horn bit into her thigh as the pack animals balked. Finally, they decided to come all at once.

The sudden loss of tension on the lead rope caused her horse to stumble. Clutching the saddlehorn, Marty screamed, and for a horrible second, she thought she was going over the edge.

Planting his feet. her horse finally caught his balance, and started down again. He moved slower this time, almost feeling his way along.

Trying to get her heart started again, Marty looked down. Past her left boot, the whole world seemed to fall away. The scattered trees at the bottom looked like toothpicks.

Tightening her hold on the saddle horn, Marty swallowed the lump in her throat. Panic threatened to overwhelm her. She could feel her heart racing. Right then, Marty wished desperately she was back in the canyon with Tucker. She wished she had never heard of the treasure, never come west at all!

Marty silently repeated a prayer she had learned as a kid. Just as she finished, her horse lurched. She heard herself scream again, a high pitched yelp.

A horrible thought occurred to her—did saddles ever come loose? She remembered hearing that a saddle that wasn't cinched up properly could come loose.

In her mind, Marty tried to recall this morning when she saddled her horse. Had she tightened the cinch enough? For the life of her, Marty couldn't even remember tightening the thing.

Her heart pounding like a runaway train, Marty looked down. She didn't want to, but she just couldn't help herself. Her heart almost jumped into her throat at the sight of the awful depths below.

Quickly she snapped her eyes forward, concentrating on looking straight ahead. Her palms were sweating so much that they were fast becoming slippery. Gritting her teeth, she forced herself to unhook one hand and dry it on her shirt front. As soon as she wiped it dry, the hand dove for the saddle horn. Drying the other hand, Marty concentrated on everything but falling.

She heard the packs scraping against rock, as the pack

horses held to the inside of the trail. Marty tried to get worked up over the fact that the packs might break open. All of a sudden, the gold didn't seem that important.

Tears came to her eyes, and Marty desperately wanted to stop. She willed her hands to pull back on the reins, but couldn't force herself to release the death grip on the saddlehorn.

It's just as well, Marty told herself. There wasn't room on the ledge to dismount once she stopped. Despite herself, Marty glanced down. Was it her imagination, or was the trail growing wider?

Hopefully, Marty looked again. Sure enough, the trail was indeed wider. Her left foot no longer hung over empty space. Just those couple of extra feet did wonders for Marty's confidence. Ahead, she could tell the trail flattened out some.

Marty's breath came easier, and the tightness left her chest. She even managed to ease her grip on the saddlehorn. For once, Marty begin to think she might get off this mountain alive.

As the steepness left the trail, Marty's horse increased his speed. The pack horses followed right along, seemingly eager to reach the bottom as quickly as possible.

The first switchback proved to be a sharp narrow turn, but Marty's horse didn't hesitate as he bent around it. Marty's boot dragged against the wall as her mount negotiated the turn.

She feared the bulkiness of the packs would give the other horses problems as they rounded the bend. The packs scraped heavily on the wall, sending a shower of dirt and rocks below. The last animal in line slipped going around the corner. His hind leg slipped over the edge of the trail. The frightened animal screamed, breaking rocks loose as he fought to stay on the trail.

The lead rope tightened, and the force of the other animals pulling gave him enough lift to scramble back onto the path.

Marty pulled up, giving the animals a respite. As the horses rested, Marty regained her composure. For a minute there, she'd been sure she was going to lose the last horse.

She looked up to where she had been. The sight gave her shivers. Even though she was already better than halfway down, Marty didn't like sitting on the side of a mountain. Lifting the reins, she urged her horse on.

The next switchback was a wide gentle turn, giving the horses no trouble. They scooted around the bend as eager to reach the bottom as Marty.

Ahead, Marty could see where the trail had been wiped out by a rock slide. The slide extended a good thirty feet to the grassy valley floor. Dejection hit Marty like a cold slap in the face. Even if she could manage to turn her horse around, she wasn't going back up the trail!

Her horse solved her problem. With a frog-like hop, he jumped out on the slope. Marty could feel the rock giving way beneath his hooves as they were swept toward the bottom.

Using his stiff front legs as brakes, the horse squatted on his haunches and slid with the flow of dirt and rock.

The pack animals, being tied on, didn't have any choice but to follow. Their shrill screams rang in Marty's ears. Feeling out of control, Marty choked on the dust being raised by the plunging animals.

Five or six feet from the bottom, Marty felt her horse squat even lower and tense his powerful muscles. With a shrill whinny, he bounded out on the flat, grassy valley floor. The lead rope cut cruelly into Marty's thigh as the pack animals were towed along.

Bucking and jumping, they were swept to the bottom.

The poor last horse was jerked to his knees and was hauled a few feet before he could scramble back onto his feet.

Marty had her hands full as she fought to control her horse and stay in the saddle at the same time. She didn't see the six men until she slammed into them.

They'd been staring at Marty in open-mouthed disbelief. When her plunging horses jumped into the middle of them, they snapped into action. They grabbed the lead ropes, controlling the animals easily.

A tall, razor-thin man with a hatchet face latched onto Marty's bridle. Her horse crow-hopped sideways a few times, but under the firm grip of the tall man, the animals settled right down.

The tall man pushed back his hat, revealing straw-colored hair. "Ma'am, you must be plumb crazy," he drawled slowly, looking up at the trail Marty came down. "If one of those pack horses fell over the edge, he'd most likely drag the whole bunch over."

"I never thought of that," Marty admitted, glad that particular thought hadn't occurred to her while she was on the trail. "One of the horses did slip though."

"That's right he did just slip, if he'd fell any further, you'd been in big trouble."

"Well, I'm down now. If you gentlemen will excuse me, I'll be on my way," Marty said, looking nervously at the men holding her pack horses.

"Just a moment, ma'am. We need to ask you a few questions," the tall man said, maintaining his hold on her reins.

Marty's eyes widened as she finally noticed the star pinned to the man's shirt. "What business do you have with me?" she asked, trying to sound forceful.

"I'm Sheriff Lane Beauford out of Durango. We just had

our bank robbed,'' the tall man said, patting Marty's horse on the neck.

"You think I had something to do with that?" Marty asked, looking horrified. "Sheriff Beauford, I do not have to sit here and listen to such accusations," she added sharply.

Sheriff Beauford dropped her reins, and raised both hands defensively. "Whoa, ma'am, I didn't think for a second that you did. I just wanted to ask you if you've seen the Tucker Evans gang."

"Huh?" Marty said, confused by the statement.

"Sorry, I guess you don't know about them," Sheriff Beauford apologized. "Tucker Evans is an infamous outlaw, we heard he was in this area." Sheriff Beauford went on to describe Tucker.

"I saw that man," Marty said, thinking quickly. "We met at a wagon train. He said he was coming this way. He was trying to trade with the settlers for fresh horses when I left."

"How do you know he was going to come this way?" Sheriff Beauford asked.

"He told me he was going to Santa Fe. He mentioned something about getting out of Colorado. He wanted me to wait and ride with him, but I didn't trust his look."

The sheriff nodded in agreement. A woman alone couldn't be too careful. "What *are* you doing out here alone?" he asked suddenly.

"I live down the trail. My husband broke his leg, and I had to go for supplies," Marty answered quickly.

Sheriff Beauford rubbed his jaw, gazing intently into Marty's face. "Alright, ma'am, you can go on home, but you best be careful. This ain't safe country," he said, motioning for his men to release her horses. "I'd be glad to send a man to escort you home."

Despite her sudden panic, Marty managed a small smile. "That's very kind, but hardly necessary. It's not far and I can manage. I'm sure you need all your men to capture this dangerous outlaw."

Sheriff Beauford scratched his head, and for an awful moment Marty thought he was going to insist on sending one of his men. "Alright, ma'am, but you be careful."

After Marty disappeared from sight, one of the deputies, a slim, wiry man in stained buckskins, approached the sheriff. "How much of that did you believe?"

"Not much, Pete," the sheriff admitted. "but since she wasn't wanted, I had to let her go."

Sheriff Beauford didn't mention it, but he dearly wanted to know just what was in those packs. It was a cinch that whatever was in those packs, it wasn't supplies. The nearest settlement in the direction from which Marty came was a long ways off. Too far to be going there for supplies.

"Do you think she lied about seeing Tucker?" Pete asked.

"I just don't know. I know whoever robbed the bank went northeast. That would be in the general area she came from. She might have seen them," Beauford answered thoughtfully.

"If you knew the thieves headed northeast, how come we came straight east?" Pete asked, pulling at the growth on his face.

"I figured if Tucker was the one who robbed our bank, he'd turn south soon. He and Weaver are both wanted in Colorado. I gambled that the tracks leading northeast were a bluff, and that soon they'd turn south for New Mexico."

Pete caught on immediately. "And this is the only trail south."

"The only one in this area, that I know of," Sheriff Beauford answered, absently staring at the cliff trail.

"Are we going up that?" Pete asked doubtfully, his eyes following the sheriff's along the face of the cliff.

"No, I don't believe so," the sheriff answered slowly. "I think we'll just wait here. Once they get out on that slide, we'll have them dead to rights. Not even Tucker could escape that one."

Chapter Seventeen

Tucker grinned down at Luke Sherrier. "What you need to do is decide how much eighty dollars means to you. Cause, when the shooting starts, I'm gonna kill you right off."

Luke Sherrier blinked and backed up a step. He hadn't counted on this man showing fight, not after he saw the odds stacked against him. Secretly, Luke marveled at the man's reckless courage. But Luke possessed his share of courage, and when they passed out plain old mule stubbornness, Luke stood in the line twice and held out both hands.

"I mean to have my money," he said, gritting his teeth.

Jacob McGilvey sensed the fight coming on. Good men, some of them his friends, were going to die, and Jacob felt responsible.

"Wait a minute," Jacob shouted, stepping between Tucker's horse and Sherrier. "There's no call for gunplay. We can work this out."

"Not unless he coughs up the money," Luke declared hotly.

All eyes swung to Tucker sitting astride the sorrel. "I ain't got more than two bits to my name," Tucker said, with a shrug.

Jacob swore miserably. He chewed his fingernails and stared into the distance. Kicking the ground, he swore under his breath. "Aw look, I feel partly responsible for this mess.

I talked these fellers into making the trade. I believed the young lady.'' Jacob didn't bother to add that mostly, he had wanted to see who was chasing Marty Flynn.

"Then maybe you should fork over the eighty bucks," Tucker said bluntly.

McGilvey frowned, his blood rebelling at the thought of parting with that much money. "You mentioned that you were chasing the girl yourself?" McGilvey asked quickly.

"She stole them packs from me," Tucker said quietly.

"Well then, when you catch her, you could see that these men get their horses back, or at least the money," McGilvey suggested hopefully.

"I don't know," Tucker said scratching his head. "I wouldn't know where to find you."

"Right here," McGilvey said promptly. "We're fixing to start a town."

"Wait a minute, Jacob," Luke Sherrier protested. "How do we know we can trust this guy? We trusted that girl, and just look where that got us."

A pained expression crossed Jacob's face, and his shoulders sagged. "If we don't hear from him in a few weeks, I'll pay the eighty dollars myself," Jacob offered, then looked to Tucker. "Do we have a deal, Mister . . . ?"

"Sure, I guess," Tucker replied, not thrilled with the idea, but it was better than a bunch of them dying.

McGilvey held out his hand, arching his eyebrows expectantly. Tucker could tell the old scot wanted a name. "Tucker Evans," Tucker supplied, taking McGilvey's hand.

The sound of the name went through Luke Sherrier like a bolt of lightning. Luke's stomach turned queasy at the thought of what he'd almost done. It was one thing to buck up against some loudmouthed yahoo, but a whole different breed of cat to take on a man like Tucker.

Luke had been set to argue some more, but now his mouth snapped shut. If only half of what Luke had heard about Tucker was true, then Luke wanted no part of the man.

"Tucker Evans, huh?" McGilvey mused worriedly. He rubbed his chin, unable to look Tucker in the face, but glanced at the outlaw out of the corner of his eyes. "Folks say you rob banks for a living?"

"That's right," Tucker replied with a shrug.

Jacob groaned. He'd just kissed that eighty big ones good-bye. "Then you admit that you rob banks?"

"No," Tucker said with a grin. "but that's sure enough what folks say about me."

Luke Sherrier's partner stepped up, speaking for the first time. "You're from Missouri?" he asked.

Tucker stared at the man, trying to recognize him. The face looked familiar, but Tucker couldn't put a name to it. "I grew up in Missouri," Tucker told him.

The man nodded, satisfied. "We can trust him. I knew his folks, although their name wasn't Evans."

"Carlin," Tucker told him. "From the look of you, you'd be a Sasser," Tucker added, recognizing the face.

"Bob Sasser," the man said, extending his hand. "I know how you got started in the outlaw business, and I wanted to tell you, a lot of us figure you done the right thing, no matter what the law thinks."

Sasser started to walk back to the wagons, then stopped. "Fact is, if you are of a mind to trade the sorrel, I got a black gelding I'd swap straight across."

"I'd be obliged," Tucker said, without hesitating. He needed a fresh horse. Sasser watched while Tucker switched the saddles. "That's a mighty fine horse," Tucker said, admiring the gelding. The black horse stood a good eighteen hands high. He had a wide deep chest and bulging, powerful hindquarters.

"Nothing wrong with that sorrel. Anyways, I'm proud to be able to do you a favor." Sasser stopped, scuffing the ground with the toe of his boot. "I know you killed ole man Masters in a fair fight. I know they made an outlaw out of you over the deal, but I wanted to tell you that most of us stood up and cheered when you bedded the ole devil down under six feet of Missouri hillside."

Sasser felt uncomfortable telling Tucker that, and hearing it embarrassed Tucker. For a moment, both of them stared at the ground, kicking stones. Suddenly, Sasser extended his hand awkwardly. Tucker took the hand and worked it like a pump handle.

"Thanks for the horse, Mister Sasser," Tucker said, mounting the black horse. "I won't forget it."

Sasser waved off Tucker's thanks. "Don't you worry about that money either. If it's going to be a problem for you to get back this way, I'll cover it for you. And don't worry about Luke, he's a good man, just awful concerned about money."

"Money's important," Tucker pointed out.

"Sure it is," Sasser replied with a dry chuckle. "Dealing with ole man Masters sure taught us all that, but I'm proud to say that I still put friends higher up on the ladder. I knew your folks well, and was sorry to hear of their passing. I know you blamed yourself for that, but no one else did."

"One person did," Tucker said softly.

Sasser started to walk away, then glanced back. "How is Deke?" he asked.

"I don't rightly know," Tucker said, his voice rough. "He looked well enough last time I saw him."

Sasser shook his head, sadly. "One of these days, you two are going to have to make up."

Tucker sat on his horse watching Sasser walk away. Sasser had been wrong, Tucker knew of one person who still blamed him for his parents death, and always would. Tucker rode away from the wagons with a heavy heart. He felt this way every time he thought of his family.

Tucker picked up the trail, wondering just how important the treasure really was. For the first time, Tucker took a long, hard look at his life. He'd robbed and stole all over the country, and now he felt ashamed of it.

He used to think he was so smart. Fooling the law and stealing had been just a big game to him. Course, Tucker had played the game as hard as he could. Now Tucker realized he wasn't a kid anymore, but he couldn't stop the game. He was trapped.

Tucker stuck to the trail more to see Marty again than to get his share of the treasure. She hadn't trusted him, that's why she ran off.

I can't blame her for that, Tucker thought bitterly. In her place, he would have done the same thing. What have I ever done to make anyone trust me, he asked himself.

Tucker remembered Bob Sasser's words ''I still put friends higher on the ladder than money,'' Tucker repeated the phrase out loud.

Well, Tucker had neither. Being broke didn't bother him, but all at once, not having any real friends did. The only people he knew were thieves and cutthroats. Oh, Tucker knew his own band was a cut above the rest, but were they his friends?

The question bothered Tucker for a long time. When he reached the cliff trail, he checked the tracks twice, and still couldn't believe Marty had actually taken the trail. But the tracks did not lie. A reckless grin came to his face. If Marty had taken the trail, so would he.

As he started down, Tucker knew this attitude was mostly what got him in trouble. Something inside him wouldn't let

Tucker back away from any challenge—he met them head on, unable to resist any dare.

The black horse took to the trail like he thought he was part mountain goat. Tucker gave the black his head, and settled back to enjoy the ride. The black negotiated the two hairpins with no trouble. He didn't even hesitate at the slide. As they slid down the slope amid a shower of dirt and rocks, Tucker saw two men step out of a grove of trees.

They leveled rifles at him, and Tucker saw a star pinned to the chest of the taller one. Gathering the reins, Tucker got ready to slap the spurs to the black and make a run for it. More men filed out of the trees, all of them armed, and none of them looking friendly.

Knowing he was caught, Tucker dropped the reins and raised his hands. As the deputies closed in around him, Tucker wondered if he would make any friends in jail.

Danny, Weaver and Hardy approached Mason's cabin with caution. They didn't trust the situation. For all they knew, Mason had gotten loose and waited inside, ready to ambush them.

Fanning out, they moved in slowly. Staying back in the trees, Hardy circled around to the back. First thing Hardy saw was the hole beside the house. In three long bounds, he crossed the open space behind the cabin, and flattened himself against the rear wall of the cabin.

Even though he moved quickly, Hardy noted the tracks. Only one man had come up through the hole. Rising up on his toes, Hardy peeked inside the cabin through the window. One look told him the cabin was empty.

Hardy glanced down at the hole leading to the root cellar with distaste. He had no desire to poke his head through that hole.

Weaver and Danny came through the house, to find Hardy

still staring at the hole. "So they got away," Weaver observed.

"One of them did," Hardy replied dryly, indicating the tracks.

"Mason's the one that got away," Weaver decided, after looking the tracks over. "You reckon the boy's still down there."

"I don't know. Why don't you look and see?" Hardy asked.

"Are you crazy? I ain't sticking my head down there," Weaver declared hotly.

Hardy chuckled, and begin to circle the cabin, going over the ground like a bloodhound. While Hardy looked around, Weaver settled down on the ground to rest. He held his rifle ready in case someone poked their head up out of the hole. In which case, Weaver was ready to tap them with the barrel of his rifle.

"Why don't you just go down there?" Danny asked.

"Well, for all we know ol' Mason is down there just waiting for us. He coulda had an extra gun stashed someplace. You stick your head down there and you'll liable to be combing slugs outta your hair for a week."

Danny got the picture and settled down to wait alongside Weaver. In ten minutes, Hardy returned. Satisfied that the place was deserted, he checked the cellar.

"The boy leave with Mason?" Weaver asked, sounding disappointed. Truth was, Weaver sort of liked Delbert, and hated to see him running with a coyote like Mason.

Hardy shook his head. "Mason left first, by himself. Someone came by later and left with the boy," Hardy replied, leading the way around to the front of the cabin.

An extra horse stood beside the two they rode to Mason's cabin. Hardy waved carelessly at the new horse. "Found him in a pasture back behind the house."

Hardy took the rope from his saddle and fashioned a crude hackamore. He slipped it on the horse, and handed the end to Danny.

"You didn't spy an extra saddle, did you?" Danny asked hopefully.

Hardy shook his head and started to mount his own horse, then stopped to look at Weaver. "The man who came and got the boy was Deke Carlin."

Weaver swore quickly, under his breath. "You think he's looking for Tucker?"

"Maybe," Hardy said. "Deke always said he would kill Tucker one day. Maybe this is the day."

Chapter Eighteen

Marty stopped. Even though there was a couple of hours of daylight remaining, she didn't feel like pushing on. Ever since leaving Sheriff Beauford and his posse, Marty felt uneasy.

She unloaded the treasure, merely unhooking the sacks and letting them fall. She had once caressed the golden pieces lovingly, but now she almost hated the stuff.

Despite everything she had learned, Marty built a fire and made coffee. She thought about cooking, but didn't feel hungry. Her stomach was tied in knots.

Marty drank her coffee, staring into the fire. She didn't notice the shadows growing longer and darkness falling. Feeding sticks to the fire, she sipped her coffee. Getting the treasure didn't feel at all like she dreamed it would be.

By rights, she should be jumping up and down, rolling in the middle of all that gold. Marty didn't feel any pride in having wealth, and she sure wasn't proud of the things she'd done to get it.

Angry with herself, Marty kicked dirt on the fire, putting out the blaze. As she unrolled her bedroll, she tried to justify her actions.

What had she done that was so bad? Nothing! All she had done was tell a few white lies. What harm could ever come of that? If she had trusted anyone, she'd probably have gotten left out in the cold just like Tucker.

"Tucker," she repeated the name, her voice sounding

loud in the stillness of the night. Marty remembered how her heart pounded while they huddled under the blanket that wild, rainy night. She'd wanted to throw her arms around him and hold him tight, but lacked the nerve to do so.

Propping herself on one elbow, Marty stared through the darkness at the black lumps of the treasure sacks. What had she done? How much had she sacrificed for a few sacks of trinkets?

Marty could see her Uncle Jack in her mind. The lessons he taught her flashed through her brain. Now they sounded hollow and empty. He taught her about everything, everything but love.

"Everybody's got to trust somebody, sometime," Tucker had said. Did he believe that? Who did he trust?

Marty slept fitfully that night. This time it wasn't the night or the fact that she was alone which bothered her. Or maybe it was that she was alone. So alone.

Well before dawn, she gave up trying to sleep. She built up her fire and sat on a log, watching the flames devour the sticks.

As the first streaks of light dimmed the stars, Marty came to a decision. Putting out the fire, Marty saddled her horse and loaded the packs. Despite the weight of the packs, she worked quickly. Her mind made up, a peace came to her mind. But as she rode out of camp, doubt crept up on her. She touched her hair nervously, unsure about what she was going to do.

Deke Carlin and Delbert broke camp at dawn. Delbert still limped as he gathered his gear. Fussing with his cinch, Deke frowned as Delbert limped to his horse. Deke felt a bit guilty about pushing the boy, but Delbert wanted to ride on.

Just before going into camp the night before, they'd found

two trails. One was Marty's, the other belonged to Tucker. Deke laughed when he saw that Marty had the treasure with her. That girl sure did beat everything—to think that Deke had worried about her.

Deke chuckled again, ignoring the strange look he got from Delbert. That girl sure was a firebrand. Deke could imagine Tucker's rage. Served him right. Let him see how it felt to get something taken from him!

Mid-morning they spotted the group of wagons. Deke took a moment to look them over, before leading Delbert down. A bearded man met them at the edge of the circle of wagons.

"Boy, we sure picked the right place to start a town, we've had a pile of visitors these past couple of days," he said, holding out his hand. "My name is McGilvey. Jacob McGilvey."

"Deke Carlin," Deke grunted, taking the hand. "My saddle partner there is Delbert Gaines."

Delbert felt proud of the way Deke called him his partner. Imitating Deke's grave expression, Delbert shook hands with the bearded settler.

"You said you had visitors. When did they pass through?" Deke asked, intent on getting down to business.

"The young lady with all the pack animals, she came by here evening before last. That outlaw feller, Tucker Evans, he passed through the next morning. Another feller came by yesterday evening. He never did give his name, but he sure asked a pile of questions about the first two," McGilvey answered, his curiosity growing by leaps and bounds.

"That last feller, was he a small man with a mean look to him?" Deke asked, repeating the description of Mason the way Delbert gave it to him.

"Shore was. Like you said, a small feller, but no one to

mess with, I can tell you that. He had the meanest looking eyes I ever did see."

Bob Sasser left the cabin he was starting to build, hurrying to join the conference. "How you been, Deke?" he asked.

"Alright, I reckon," Deke grunted, looking the man over closely. "How's things with you, Bob?" The name coming to him all of a sudden.

Sasser shrugged. The kids were sick, and the wife was harping about not having a house yet. All in all, things were just about normal. "I seen your little brother the other day. He looked well."

"He won't be well for long, not if I catch up to him," Deke growled.

"You still blaming him for what happened back in Missouri?" Sasser asked. "He was just a boy at the time."

"He was old enough to get our pa killed!"

"Tucker didn't kill your pa. The Masters clan done that," Sasser reminded gently. "You shouldn't blame him for that."

"He hasn't done much since then to redeem himself," Deke replied testily, then changed the subject. "What was the story between him and the girl?"

Bob Sasser chuckled, shaking his head. "It's quite a story, alright," he said. "She claimed they was married, he said they wasn't and that she stole the horses and packs. Between the two of them, they owe us eighty dollars." Sasser looked up at Deke. "Are they married?"

"Not that I know of, but with them two you can never tell. One's 'bout as crazy as the other," Deke replied. He fished out four twenty-dollar gold pieces from his pocket and handed them to Sasser. "I'll pay their debts."

Bob took the money, knowing Deke would be upset if he didn't. "Come up to the fire, we'll talk for a spell. Catch up on old times," Sasser offered.

Deke shook his head, and started to decline the offer, but McGilvey cut him off. "He won't do it, nobody ever wants to stop and sit. That's the trouble with the world, everybody's in such a blasted hurry."

McGilvey's remark brought a smile to Deke's weather-beaten face. "Thanks for the invite, but I just ain't got the time right now. I'd be obliged if you could take care of my partner for a few days though. He's been shot."

Deke saw Delbert about to protest, but overruled him. "Look, son, I can't have you slowing me down." Deke saw the hurt spring to Delbert's eyes, and was sorry for what he said. "What I mean is, you're still limping. I don't like that, your leg should be about healed up by now. You best stay off of it for a few days, or you'll have that limp the rest of your life."

Delbert didn't say a word as McGilvey led his horse into the circle of wagons. He didn't even look back or wave at Deke.

"You hurt the boy's feelings," Sasser observed.

"I know, but I am worried about the leg. Besides, I got to travel fast. I gotta catch Tucker and that girl before Mason does!"

Chapter Nineteen

Hardy pulled up so quickly that Weaver's horse bumped into him. Weaver started cussing, but Hardy silenced him with a desperate hiss. "I smell wood smoke," Hardy explained.

Both Weaver and Danny lifted their heads, testing the wind with their noses, but neither could smell the smoke. They didn't question Hardy though. Sometimes Weaver thought his umber-skinned companion had a sixth sense.

Tying their horses, the three outlaws proceeded on foot. In the middle of a maze of fallen trees, they found three men in a tiny camp. Spread out on a blanket between them was a large pile of money.

"That's the men from the posse out of Silver City," Danny whispered excitedly.

"Aw, horse hooey," Weaver grumbled, rubbing his eyes as he stared at the men, trying to see if the kid was right. It seemed like years since they stopped that stage robbery down in New Mexico.

"They boy is right," Hardy whispered.

Weaver's eyes left the faces of the men, and strayed to the pile of money. An unspoken agreement passed between Weaver and Hardy. As one, they crept closer to the camp.

Not quite sure what they were doing, Danny followed cautiously. The two older men took positions behind fallen logs where they could cover the camp. Weaver jerked Danny down beside him. The big outlaw leveled his rifle at the camp and jacked a shell into the firing chamber. The sound of metal grating on metal sounded loud in the stillness of the mountain forest.

The three men in the camp stopped counting the money, looking like statues carved from stone. "That's real good," Weaver called. "You know, you boys may be uglier than Jacob's dog, but you're showing some sense, keep it up and you just might stay breathing. Now, stand up slowly," Weaver instructed.

Hardy left his position, moving carefully so as not to block Weaver's line of fire and approached the camp. Covering them with his own rifle, Hardy took their pistols, shoving them in his belt.

Holding his rifle one-handed, Hardy knelt beside the pile of money. One of the posse members, a hatchet-faced man with buck teeth, thought he saw a chance. He drew back his leg to smash a kick in Hardy's face.

Hardy lashed out with his rifle, catching the man's support leg on the side of the knee. Crying out in pain, the man fell heavily. He lay on the ground, groaning and clutching his knee.

Ignoring the man, Hardy pushed the money to the center of the blanket. Gathering up all four corners, he tied them in a knot, making an effective sack.

"Lay down on your bellies with your hands behind your heads," he instructed, watching as the grumbling posse members complied.

"Grab one of their saddles," Danny called out, thinking of his sore backside.

Tucking the money under his arm, Hardy snatched up one of their saddles. He backed away, keeping the three prone men in sight.

"You boys just lay there and contemplate your sins,"

Weaver told them. "I wouldn't even think about moving till morning."

Hardy took up a defensive position, while Weaver and Danny took the saddle and the money. Soon, Hardy heard his friends scattering the posse members' horses as they made their escape.

Hardy took a piece of jerky from his pocket and chewed the tough meat while he waited. Fifteen minutes passed before one of the posse members decided it was safe to move. As the man started to rise, Hardy put a bullet over the man's shoulder within inches of his ear. Cursing wildly, the man flopped back down to the ground.

Using the sound of the curses to mask his movements, Hardy ghosted back to his horse. He led his horse wide around the camp. Once he was out of earshot, he mounted and rode hard to catch his friends. Ten minutes later, he found them, waiting. When he saw Hardy, Weaver let out a whoop, holding up the bag of money. They were a joyous lot as they rode away. None of them knew that their actions of the past hour would have such disastrous results.

Tucker sat on the ground, his back against a log, and his hands tied in front of him. The only concession to comfort Sheriff Beauford had allowed.

Beauford sat across from Tucker, asking the same questions over and over. Beauford showed the patience of Job and the tenacity of a bulldog as he stuck to his task.

"Where's the money from the bank in Durango? We know you held the place up. It'll go easier on you if you give us the money."

"You deaf or something? How many times do I have to tell you; I never robbed your bank, and I don't know where the money is," Tucker replied tiredly.

"Where is your gang?" the sheriff asked.

"Gang? Do you see a gang around here?"

"Alright, suppose you tell me just what you are doing in this part of the country?" the sheriff asked, rubbing his tired eyes.

"I done told you; this lady hired us to lead her to Black Canyon. She had a treasure map. Well, we found the gold, and she cut out without giving us our share. That's why I was following her."

"How did she get past you with all of that gold?"

"She put something in the food to knock us out," Tucker explained, growing tired of the game.

"Us? So you weren't by yourself?" Sheriff Beauford demanded, rising to his feet.

"No. Three of my friends went into the mountains with me."

"Two of those friends wouldn't be Oshea Weaver and Hardy Scranton? Would they?" Beauford asked, his tone growing derisive.

"Maybe," Tucker admitted sullenly, "but we never robbed your crummy bank. I promise you that. So there is no need for you to hold me."

"You are wanted in Colorado, remember? Even if I can't prove you robbed our bank, it's still my duty to turn you over to the U.S. marshal."

Tucker cursed under his breath. To think he was going to be caught and jailed for a bank he didn't rob.

"Sheriff, someone's coming," one of the lookouts called softly.

"Coming down the cliff trail?" Sheriff Beauford called back, urgency creeping into his normally calm voice.

"No, sir. Coming in from the south. I think it's the woman with all the packs."

Tucker felt a quick stab of hope. Marty could set them straight. She could tell them he had been with her in the mountains while the bank in Durango was being robbed. But would she?

Tucker honestly didn't know, but then he realized it really didn't matter. As the sheriff pointed out, Tucker was wanted in Colorado. Either way, he was going to jail.

"Good day to you, Miss. Did you lose your way?" Sheriff Beauford greeted Marty politely.

"No, I just got to thinking that perhaps I gave you the wrong idea. Mister Evans could not have robbed your bank. He was with me in the mountains at the time. We found a stash of Spanish gold, that's what's in the packs."

"That's not the same story you told me yesterday. Then you claimed you met Tucker at a wagon camp," Sheriff Beauford reminded her.

Crestfallen, Marty remembered saying that now. "But you must believe me, I'm telling the truth this time!" she pleaded.

"You were lying before, but you are telling the truth now," the sheriff mimicked, a trace of sarcasm in his voice. "Lady, I don't know what your game is, but I don't think I can believe either one of your stories."

"Can I at least talk to Tucker?"

It was obvious from the sheriff's expression that he didn't care for the idea, but he gave in to the pleading look on Marty's face. "Okay, but don't try to slip him a gun or knife, I'll be watching you," the sheriff warned, motioning for his men to give them some room. Sheriff Beauford crossed his arms, and took a position, leaning against a tree where he could watch them.

His deputy, Pete, squatted beside the sheriff. "I think she's telling the truth this time. Her story matches up with Tucker's," Pete suggested.

"Likely you're right, but that don't change the fact that

Tucker is wanted. I'm bound by duty to bring him in,'' Sheriff Beauford insisted.

"Sure you are," Pete agreed. "But you are also duty bound to find the home folk's money. And they are the ones who pay our salaries."

Sheriff Beauford didn't say anything. He leaned back, liking the feel of the rough bark against his back. He knew what Pete had in mind.

"If Tucker didn't rob our bank, then we best get to finding out who did. We can't be dragging a prisoner all over the mountains. We'd never catch up to the ones that did rob our bank," Pete argued. "Folks back home sure can't afford to lose all that money."

Sheriff Lane Beauford knew deep down Pete was right. Tucker's story and Marty's second one did match. Beauford had little doubt but what they said was true.

It just galled him to let a man like Tucker go. But that's exactly what it boiled down to. Either he took Tucker in, and kissed off any chance of recovering the town's money, or he could cut Tucker loose and go after the real thieves.

Marty sat down beside Tucker. He showed her his bound hands, grinning ruefully. "I tried to tell them they had the wrong man, but they wouldn't believe me," Marty apologized.

Tucker lowered his hands and shrugged. "It doesn't matter," he replied.

"Oh, I feel responsible for all this," Marty wailed. "If I hadn't taken the treasure and ran off, none of this would ever have happened."

"It's not your fault," Tucker said, raising his bound hands to wipe the tears from her face. "If I hadn't robbed those banks, none of this would matter now," he added bitterly.

"I should never have left you all, but I thought you might

try to take the treasure from me. Now I wish I had never even seen the stuff,'' Marty said, taking Tucker's hands in her own.

Tucker's face softened, and for a second he didn't know what to say. Her eyes were pleading with him for forgiveness. ''Aw, don't worry yourself about it. You probably done the right thing. If you would have trusted me, things might have turned out just like you feared,'' Tucker said, trying to give her comfort. ''Besides, if I'd been paying better attention, they might not have caught me.''

Marty flinched, her eyes no longer willing to meet Tucker's. ''They knew you were coming,'' Marty explained in a small voice. She watched Tucker carefully, fearful that he might explode at any minute. ''I told them you were behind me. I wanted to slow you down some.''

To her shock, Tucker laughed. ''Well, you sure slowed me down. You should'a kept going, you could be a long ways away by now.''

Marty lowered her eyes, looking at her hands around Tucker's. ''I found out I didn't want to go alone,'' she said, then raised her head to look him in the eye.

Tucker was shocked speechless. While he floundered around for something to say, Sheriff Beauford interrupted them.

Marty dropped Tucker's hands as she shot to her feet. ''Sheriff, on those horses is a fortune in gold and diamonds. You and your town can have it, if you'll just let Tucker go.''

Sheriff Beauford had been coming to turn Tucker loose, so the posse could get on with the business of catching the bank robbers and recovering the town's money. But now he changed his mind. Beauford didn't like being pushed. His men were pushing him to let Tucker go, and now so was Marty Flynn.

Sheriff Lane Beauford decided not to take it any more. He had six men, two of them could take Tucker to Durango. Four men. The sheriff knew it was foolish to go after a bunch of outlaws with only four men. The odds would be about even, but the outlaws would be desperate to escape.

Sheriff Beauford set his jaw firmly. He'd wait here till morning on the odd chance that Tucker and his girl had concocted their story. If Tucker had been in on the Durango bank robbery, his men would be coming down the cliff trail soon.

Sheriff Beauford set his feet firmly and crossed his arms across his chest. "That sounds a lot like you are trying to bribe me, Miss," he scolded. "I can't let Tucker go, so you just keep your treasure. Tucker's going to jail and that's final!"

Chapter Twenty

Delbert ate the meal offered to him by the settlers in silence. A couple of times, Jacob McGilvey tried to start a conversation with the youngster, but all he got in return was a grunt. Giving up, Jacob left the boy in peace and returned to work on his cabin.

Delbert looked past the wagons in the direction Deke Carlin took. In a way, Delbert felt a vast relief to be left behind. Mason frightened Delbert. Right about now, working on his pa's farm looked mighty appealing to Delbert.

A part of Delbert wanted to go home, but he wasn't going to do that. Delbert was going to see this through. Somehow, Delbert felt a sense of duty. He'd helped Mason, and now Delbert felt he should do something to stop Mason. Delbert felt a chill as he remembered the look in Mason's eyes when the small man said he would take care of Marty Flynn.

Bitterly, Delbert wished Deke Carlin had taken him along. Anything was better than going alone. Deke hadn't trusted him, Delbert knew that. Mason had just used the youngster, then left him to fend for himself. Delbert had enough. Tossing his plate and fork on the ground, Delbert rose and looked off in the distance.

He couldn't see Deke, of course, but he could track him. Couldn't he? For the first time in his life, Delbert took a look at things honestly. Seeing the world for the way it was, instead of the way he dreamed it to be.

Delbert could track. But deep down, he didn't know if

he was good enough to follow a trail for what might be days on end without losing it. Of course, there would be four trails, counting Deke's. With all those tracks on the ground, surely Delbert could stick to the trail.

Slowly and carefully, Delbert took his pistol from the holster. He checked the loads, and replaced the weapon. He didn't twirl the gun, as he had liked to do in the past. Delbert had practiced with that gun for hours, telling himself he was as good as the best.

Now, Delbert didn't feel so sure. It was one thing to shoot at a bunch of cans and dream. The thought of facing someone who might shoot back was altogether different.

Delbert knew he could hit what he shot at. Would that be enough? Delbert hoped so, knowing he would soon find out.

Walking slowly, Delbert concentrated on not limping. The pain in his leg almost gave him comfort. Delbert drew strength from his pain.

Bob Sasser dropped his ax, sprinting to cut the young man off. As Delbert started to mount his horse, Sasser grabbed the lad by the shoulder. "Don't do it, son," Sasser said seriously. "Nobody expects this from you, there's no reason to go and get yourself killed."

"You're wrong, Mister Sasser, I expect something from myself. I've got to see this mess through to the end. I shot off my big mouth, now I've got to pay my dues."

"A boy should have the right to run off at the mouth without having to die for it," Bob Sasser argued.

Delbert didn't reply, he merely looked at Sasser with a determined look. "Stop and think about what you are doing." Sasser told him.

"I have thought about it. I thought about it all morning. I feel like I'm partly to blame for bringing Mason here, and I've got to try and stop him."

"Hogwash!" Sasser exploded. "Tucker's a grown man. He can take care of himself."

"It's not Tucker I'm worried about, it's the girl," Delbert said quietly.

"Alright, son, if you are bound and determined to do this, I won't stop you, but just be careful," Sasser said, giving Delbert a fatherly pat on the shoulder.

"You know son, this is just how Tucker got started. He was a boy, not even as old as you. He went looking for a man who cheated his pa out of their farm. Well, when it was all said and done, Tucker's pa was dead, and Tucker was an outlaw. All because Tucker felt like you do now. My advice to you is just let it lay. Things have a way of working out for the best all by themselves."

Delbert mounted his horse, and looked down at the older man. "Thank you for all your help, Mister Sasser. I'll be going now," Delbert said, swinging his horse around.

Picking up the trail presented no problems. And as he followed the tracks, Delbert's confidence rose. This might not be as hard as he thought. Soon, Delbert could identify the different tracks. He concentrated on Deke's and Mason's.

All afternoon Delbert stuck with his task. Several times, he pulled up, staring east in the direction of his father's farm. Once, he even swung his horse around. He sat there for a long time. Desperately, Delbert wished to go home.

"We'll stop here," Hardy decided. "Not far ahead is a cliff. The trail down is very steep. I would not want to try it in the darkness."

Weaver only grunted, just happy that the son of a gun had finally stopped. They'd put in one long day. Weaver unsaddled his horse, then helped Danny with his. Danny's arm still bothered him, making it hard for the lad to work the cinch on his saddle.

"Let's count the money," Danny suggested eagerly. "If we don't get our share of the treasure, at least we won't be broke."

"No. We can count it later," Hardy said roughly. Something about the money bothered him. Where did it come from?

With the morning, they were up and moving. In the gray light of early morning, they read the tracks at the top of the cliff trail, totally unaware that they were watched from below.

Triumphantly, Sheriff Beauford lowered his field glasses. His hunch had been right all along. The sheriff had no doubts, the men at the top of the cliff had to be the ones that robbed his bank. If they were Tucker's men or not was all that remained to be seen.

Sheriff Beauford glanced around the camp in the grove of trees, making sure everyone was under cover. He planned to take these men the same way he captured Tucker. While they were on the steep slide, busy controlling their horses.

Sheriff Beauford put one of his men to watch Tucker. "You make a sound or a move to warn them, and he'll shoot. We'll open up on the men up there, and you'll all be dead," the sheriff warned.

Feeling a helpless rage, Tucker watched as his men started down the cliff trail into Sheriff Beauford's waiting trap.

Tucker silently hoped that Danny would keep his wits. If the hot-headed youngster tried anything, Beauford's men would open fire.

Chapter Twenty-one

Delbert awoke, knowing he was in trouble. Last night he lost the trail, trying to make up time by traveling in the dark. Hours after losing the trail, he finally gave up trying to find the tracks again, and simply collapsed.

Curled in a ball, Delbert huddled against a log and slept. He had slept too soundly. Now, three men stood over him. All three carried rifles, but didn't point them at Delbert. Despite the fact that their rifles pointed toward the ground, the men still frightened Delbert. None of them looked to have bathed or shaved in weeks, and they all wore a harsh angry expression.

"You seen three men? One of them a big fella, a kid and an Indian-looking guy?" one of the three asked.

"No," Delbert answered slowly. He had seen these men before, but couldn't place them. "I haven't seen them. Why are you looking for them?" Delbert asked, recognizing the description as Tucker's men.

"They took some money from us."

Suddenly, Delbert recognized the three men facing him. They were the men who came by his father's farm looking for Tucker. "You are the guys from that posse," Delbert blurted out without thinking.

The leader, a slim man with buck teeth, snapped his rifle up to cover Delbert. "How do you know us?" he demanded, peering at Delbert intently.

Delbert shrank back, a little shook at the violence of the

question. ''You came by my father's farm right after the bank in Del Norte was robbed.''

As he spoke, Delbert's eyes widened as the impact of what he said soaked in. ''You're the guys that robbed the bank in Del Norte!'' he sputtered.

''That's right,'' the buck-toothed man said with a sinister-looking smile. ''And Tucker's men took it away from us. Now we want it back. But first we got to do something about you.'' Bucktooth smiled apologetically. ''After all, we can't have you running around telling every lawman you meet about us.''

''I wouldn't tell,'' Delbert whispered.

''I just can't take that chance.''

As he spoke, the buck-toothed man raised his rifle to his shoulder. Still smiling that icy smile, he sighted in on Delbert's thin chest.

Sheriff Beauford's harsh challenge rang in their ears as the three outlaws swept down the rockslide at breakneck speed. Danny wanted to slap the spurs to his horse, but vividly remembered what happened the last time he had one of those impulses.

Dropping his reins, he raised his hands, at the same time noticing Hardy and Weaver doing the same thing. Weaver glanced over to make sure the kid wasn't going to try anything. When he saw Danny's hands in the air, Weaver gave the kid a grim smile.

Sheriff Beauford's men worked quickly. In minutes, they pulled the outlaws from their mounts, took their guns and tied their hands. Lining the outlaws up, the deputies marched them into the grove of trees.

Thinking the danger was past, Tucker's guard turned to watch the arrest. He failed to see Tucker open Marty's clutch purse and take her derringer.

Tucker slipped the small gun into his vest pocket, then watched as his men were pushed into the camp. "Howdy boys, glad you could make it," Tucker called loudly. Tucker waved his bound hands at his men.

"Sit down, Tucker, and be quiet," Sheriff Beauford warned in a low voice. The sheriff motioned for Tucker's men to sit on the ground opposite Tucker.

With his hands bound, Weaver had trouble sitting. He made a couple of experimental squats, but couldn't get all the way down. Stepping forward, one of the deputies gave Weaver a shove. With a loud grunt, Weaver hit the ground on his backside, then flipped over backwards.

For a minute, he flopped around on the ground like a fish out of water, then finally managed to heave himself into a sitting position. His face red as a setting sun, Weaver glared at his tormentor. "You meat-headed fool, I oughta . . . " Weaver blustered, but Sheriff Beauford silenced him with a look of pure fire.

The sheriff paced between the outlaws, holding his rifle close to his chest. In his other hand, he carried the money tied up in the blanket.

He stopped suddenly, pointing his rifle at Danny. The color drained from the youngster's face, but he held his composure. "Tell me where you guys got all this money," the sheriff demanded, shaking the money in Danny's face.

Danny looked across at Tucker. "Just tell them the truth," Tucker advised.

"Well, we went up in the mountains with Miss Flynn to find this treasure. After we found the gold . . . " Danny paused, not sure what to say about Marty leaving with the treasure. "Some of our horses ran off. Miss Flynn and Tucker went on ahead. The rest of us stayed behind to round up the rest of the horses," Danny finished, uncomfortably.

"I didn't ask about that. I asked you about this," Sheriff Beauford growled, shoving the money into Danny's face.

"We took that from three men yesterday," Danny said defiantly. "We didn't steal it."

"You just said you did," Beauford countered savagely. "It doesn't make any difference whether you take it from a bank or three men in the woods—it's still stealing."

Disgusted, the sheriff resumed his pacing. "You men agree with the kid's story?" he asked.

"That's about the way I remember it," Weaver replied in an offhand way. Hardy nodded silently.

Sheriff Beauford paced back and forth a few more times. Pivoting quickly, he walked away, slapping the money against his, thigh. He tossed the money to his deputy, Pete. "Count this, then put it in my saddlebag," he barked.

While Pete went to count the money, Sheriff Beauford told one of his other deputies, "Go get the horses ready. We'll be moving out soon."

"What about the lady's stuff?" the deputy asked, pointing to where Marty sat beside Tucker.

"Load it on her horses," Sheriff Beauford said. "I'll go talk to her."

"Sheriff, me and the boys have been thinking," the deputy said, fidgeting uncomfortably. "We looked in those packs and what they said is true, them packs are full of gold. You should see the stuff!"

"And you thought, we should help ourselves to a part of it," Sheriff Beauford replied, his voice whipping across the air like a lash. "Look, we are here to uphold the law. As far as I'm concerned, that treasure belongs to the young lady. It's our duty to see that she keeps it!"

The deputy squirmed under the sting of the sheriff's words. "I'll go get the horses ready," he said, leaving at a run.

Pete came back with the money held loosely in the blanket. "Sheriff, there's about twice as much money here as was taken from our bank," he said. "Where do you suppose the rest came from?"

"I heard that the bank in Del Norte was robbed. They probably hit that one too," the sheriff reasoned. "When we get back to town, I want you to ride over to Del Norte. Find out the details of their robbery."

"I could leave now," the deputy suggested. "Sure would save me a lot of time riding."

Sheriff Beauford's brow furrowed as he thought about it. He hated to loose even one man. Even tied up, Tucker and his men were still very dangerous. The sheriff wasn't forgetting about Marty Flynn either. He didn't know what to think of her, or where she stood. One thing the sheriff knew, Marty Flynn had a lot of gumption, she might just up and decide to help Tucker.

She stayed close to Tucker, and they looked mighty friendly to the sheriff. He wouldn't be surprised if she up and tried to help him escape.

"Alright, Pete, take off. Just hurry back, and be careful."

As Pete rode away, the sheriff saw Tucker and Marty put their heads close together. They were whispering something to each other.

Chapter Twenty-two

Mason watched Sheriff Beauford lead his party out of the grove of trees. Mason slipped down the cliff trail during the night. He watched with great satisfaction while Tucker's men were being arrested.

Following at a safe distance, Mason tagged along behind the procession as they headed for Durango. Mason felt sure Marty would take the treasure and turn south soon. But as the miles fell behind them, Mason became less sure. Marty rode close to Tucker and showed no signs of breaking away.

Confused and disgusted, Mason reined his horse in, letting them pull farther ahead. He took out the makin's and built himself a smoke. Mason knew he should just write this one off. He took two quick puffs off his cigarette and tossed it aside.

That treasure belonged to him! Mason had spent years looking for it, and the treasure was rightfully his. Fire blazing in his eyes, Mason spurred his horse savagely. He rode hard, swinging wide to get around them.

A few minutes later Deke dismounted at the same spot. He picked up the cigarette discarded by Mason. Deke snuffed out the smoke, and checked around for a fire. Sure that the cigarette hadn't started anything else to burning, Deke climbed back on his horse.

Deke didn't have any idea who the people were that Tucker rode with. Not that he really cared. As long as Tucker and Marty were together.

Deke had no doubts about Mason. Deke could read the smaller man's thoughts, just like he was inside Mason's head. Mason wanted that treasure, and he wasn't about to give it up. Not without a fight.

Deke spurred his horse, hurrying to catch up with Mason. As Deke hurried, he lost some of his usual caution. He never even heard the shot.

Tucker and Marty rode side by side, talking quietly. "I'll use the money from the treasure to hire you the best lawyer," Marty promised.

Tucker shook his head. "It won't do any good. They have us dead to rights," he said. "You do what you started to do. Go to Santa Fe, when you get there look up Deke Carlin. You can trust him."

"What's the story between you two?" Marty asked. "I mean first he says he is going to kill you, then he tells me I can trust you. Even though you know he is going to try and kill you, you risk your life to save his. Then you tell me I can trust him."

Tucker laughed nervously. "We are brothers," he said. "My real name is Tucker Evan Carlin."

"Brothers!" Marty exclaimed. "If you are brothers, why does he want to kill you?"

"Deke blames me for our parents' death," Tucker replied, with a heavy shrug. "He thinks the life I lead brings disgrace to our family."

"How did you get started being an outlaw?"

"It's a long story," Tucker replied.

"We've got a lot of time," Marty encouraged.

Before Tucker could reply, a single shot rang out. The suddenness of it shook them all. As the sound of the shot died away, a cry of pain broke the stillness.

Delbert closed his eyes, his hands shaking. Any second, he expected to feel a bullet smashing through his body, tearing out his life as it went. As his body tensed, Delbert's ears strained to hear the shot which did not come.

Hopefully, Delbert opened his eyes. Bucktooth hadn't changed his mind, he was just prolonging the moment. The sight of his sneering face set Delbert's blood to boiling. Delbert decided he wasn't going to stand by meekly while his life was blasted away by this grinning idiot.

Throwing himself backwards, Delbert clawed frantically for his pistol. He felt a bullet whip a hot lash along his neck. Delbert's first shot missed Bucktooth, hitting the man beside him.

A shot rang from the distance, right on the heels of Delbert's. The bullet hit Bucktooth, slamming him down on top of Delbert.

The third man hesitated for just a second. Then he snapped into action. As he wheeled to face his unknown attacker, a bullet knocked him to the ground.

Delbert pushed Bucktooth off of him and climbed to his feet. Delbert's hand shook so bad that he dropped his gun. Drawing a deep breath, Delbert bent over to pick up his fallen gun. As he straightened, a short, broad man led his horse up to Delbert.

"What's going on here? Looked like they was fixing to gun you down in cold blood," the buckskin-clad man said, stooping to check the fallen men.

"They was," Delbert replied, still badly shaken. "They robbed the bank in Del Norte."

"Is that right?" the man replied, rocking back on his heels and scratching his chin. "I was just on my way to Del Norte to check into that. I'm Pete Hunt, a deputy out of Durango. We just had our bank robbed," Pete finished, rising from the fallen men.

"Are they dead?" Delbert asked, feeling sick.

"They sure are," Pete replied shortly. "How do you know these guys are the ones that robbed the bank in Del Norte?"

"They said so," Delbert said quickly. "They said Tucker Evans' men took the money from them."

Pete rubbed his jaw. Wasn't anything ever cut and dried anymore? Delbert's story backed up what Tucker's men claimed. "How come they was gonna kill you?"

"They knew I was part of the posse out of Del Norte," Delbert replied, his chest swelling with pride. Then he deflated suddenly. "I also opened my big mouth. When I realized they had to be the ones that robbed our bank, I said so."

"That'd do it," Pete agreed. "We got the money from your bank. If you want to come with me, you can pick it up."

Chapter Twenty-three

Sheriff Beauford stopped the column, his eyes straying in the direction of the shot. No doubt but that somebody was in trouble.

After some discussion, the sheriff sent two of his men to check out the mysterious shot. Sheriff Beauford worried that he had only two men besides himself to guard four prisoners, and watch Marty Flynn.

He started the column moving again. The sheriff kept back, where he could watch the whole bunch. The way Tucker kept glancing back over his shoulder, Sheriff Beauford had a hunch the outlaw knew something about the shot.

"Just keep looking straight ahead, and no talking," Sheriff Beauford warned.

As the time passed, the sheriff became more and more worried. His men should have caught back up by now. Looking back down the trail, the sheriff decided to stop. The horses could use a rest, and they could wait here until the two missing deputies caught up with them.

After an hour passed, and still no sign of the deputies, the sheriff paced back and forth, almost frantic. He should have sent more than two men. Sheriff Beauford hadn't, because he didn't want to take a chance on losing his prisoners. The sheriff admitted to himself that he wanted the fame of being the man to finally capture Tucker.

The sheriff called his two remaining deputies to him. "Something's gone wrong," he said. "I want you to go back and check it out. Be careful and hurry back. I don't trust this bunch.''

After the deputies left, Sheriff Beauford lined his prisoners and Marty Flynn up and sat them down. ''You folks just sit still and we'll get along fine. Anybody makes a fast move and it will be their last.''

The time grated by slowly with no one talking. With each passing minute, the sheriff became more nervous. Watching him pace, Tucker fingered the derringer in his vest pocket. He felt sure he could use the small gun and escape.

Now Tucker's freedom didn't seem that important to him. Maybe the best thing was to take his medicine and get it over with. His old way of life no longer sounded exciting. Western justice was notoriously lenient. Tucker figured he could get off with five years at the most.

Tucker looked at the young woman sitting beside him, and suddenly he wanted to be free. He started to draw the derringer. What kind of life could he offer a woman like Marty? On the run all the time, knowing any day might be the one he was arrested or killed. Slowly, Tucker's hand fell away from the gun.

Tucker's eyes widened as he saw Mason stalking up behind Sheriff Beauford. Hearing Mason's steps, the sheriff turned, hoping to see his deputies returning. When he saw Mason, the sheriff relaxed. Too late, he saw the gun.

When his eyes saw the gun, Sheriff Beauford reacted swiftly. He whipped his rifle up, but not swift enough. Mason took his time and squeezed off a shot. The bullet swept the sheriff backward like a giant hand.

As Mason cocked his pistol intent on finishing off Sheriff Beauford, Tucker jerked the derringer from his pocket. Earing back the hammers, Tucker fired both shots at the same time.

Mason fell to one knee, a snarl on his lips. Dropping the

gun, Tucker launched himself in a low dive at Mason. Despite his wrists being tied together, Tucker grabbed Mason's gun.

Tucker's weight bowled them both over, as they fought for control of the pistol. Mason tried to knee Tucker in the groin.

Tucker twisted away from the knee, forcing the pistol away from his body. Mason's face contorted with hate and fury, as he sought to aim the pistol at Tucker.

Tucker had both hands wrapped around the barrel of Mason's gun. Slowly, Tucker forced the muzzle of the gun toward the smaller man's stomach. With a last savage push, Tucker rammed the pistol deep into Mason's belly. Tucker's fingers found the trigger and squeezed.

The shot sounded like a dull boom, the sound muffled by Mason's clothing. Slowly, Mason's hands relaxed and the pistol came free in Tucker's hands.

Tucker pushed himself up off of Mason. He still held the gun in both hands by the barrel, when he heard the sound of a pistol being cocked behind him. "Drop the pistol, Tucker," Sheriff Beauford ordered, his voice choked with pain.

Tucker let the gun fall before turning around. Sheriff Beauford sat propped up on one elbow. He held a gun in the other hand. The sheriff's face was pinched and drawn, but the gun in his hand remained rock steady.

"Go sit with the others," Sheriff Beauford ordered, struggling to stand. He held his free hand over his side, trying to staunch the flow of blood.

Once Tucker was back in his place beside the others, the sheriff relaxed. He sat back down, and pulled the tail of his shirt from his jeans. The bullet hit him low down on the left side, just above the hip bone.

Holding the gun with one hand, the sheriff stuck the tail

of his shirt in his mouth. Holding the shirt with his teeth, he ripped a piece from the shirt, and slapped it over the wound.

"I could help you with that," Weaver offered.

"You'd like that, wouldn't you. Don't even think about it, I'm not about to let you get that close," the sheriff snapped.

"We wouldn't try anything," Weaver promised. "Tucker just saved your life, in case you forgot."

Sheriff Beauford's face turned a little red, but he set his jaw firmly. "I haven't forgot that, I'm just wondering why he did it."

"Maybe I just naturally like you," Tucker commented, watching the sheriff attempt to bandage himself. "Or maybe it's just that I have such respect for lawmen."

"Yeah, I bet," The sheriff grunted.

His crude bandaging job done, Sheriff Beauford leaned back against a tree. He put an unreadable expression on his face, and settled down to wait. For an hour the sheriff didn't say a word. He sat still as death, his pistol never wavering.

Without warning, the sheriff slumped forward, the gun spilling from his hand. A quick look passed between Tucker and his men. Looking back to Sheriff Beauford, Tucker struggled to his feet.

Tucker found the sheriff's knife and handed it to Marty. After a second's hesitation, she sawed through the bonds holding Tucker's hands.

"Cut the others loose," Tucker instructed, rolling the sheriff over. While Marty freed the others, Tucker inspected the sheriff's wound.

The bullet tore a jagged hole in Sheriff Beauford's side. Lifting the sheriff gently, Tucker looked for an exit hole. He found the sheriff's back smooth and unblemished. The bullet was lodged in the sheriff's body.

Weaver lumbered over, rubbing his wrists. "How's it look?" the big man asked, peering over Tucker's shoulder.

"I don't know," Tucker replied, moving aside to let the more experienced Weaver in. "He sure has bled a lot," Tucker said, pointing to the blood-soaked patch over the wound.

Weaver nodded grimly, kneeling beside the wounded sheriff. "He might have a chance. The bullet hit low and off to the side. A few inches over and all we could have done is started digging. If he's going to have a chance, we best stop the bleeding."

"What can we do to help?" Marty asked, worry sounding in her voice.

Weaver only grunted, busy trying to stop the flow of blood. "Get me some mud," he barked, taking his hat off, and tossing it aside. Already, Weaver's hands were stained bright red.

"Mud?" Tucker asked, automatically glancing around for a damp spot.

"Hurry up! We ain't got all day, and neither does he," Weaver shouted.

Tucker pulled the sheriff's knife from the tree trunk where Marty stuck it after cutting the men free. Kneeling down at a bare patch of ground beside a fir tree, Tucker began loosening the dirt with the knife.

Wordlessly, Hardy took a canteen from a saddle, and tossed it to Tucker. Pouring the water on the loose dirt, Tucker began mixing the mud with his hands.

"You 'bout done over there?" Weaver called urgently.

Scooping up a handful of the mud, Tucker carried it over to Weaver. The big outlaw had washed out the patch from Sheriff Beauford's shirt and laid it back over the bullet hole. Weaver took the mud from Tucker, and began packing it over the wound.

"Aren't you afraid of getting dirt in the wound?" Marty asked. "I always heard you were supposed to keep an injury clean."

"If we don't stop the bleeding, we won't have to worry about that," Weaver said. "I've seen Indians do this, they seemed to get along fine."

Weaver finished packing the mud and stepped back. "That's all I can do for now. The mud should dry and keep the bleeding under control," he said, shooting Tucker a questioning look.

Tucker saw the look and understood it. "You guys go ahead. Help Marty get her treasure to Santa Fe. I'll stay with the sheriff," he told them.

"No, sir, if you ain't going, then neither am I," Weaver declared hotly. "Besides, what do you know about treating a wounded man? You'd likely kill him just trying to help."

Tucker smiled, seeing his men, almost for the first time. They all wanted to be off, but wouldn't leave without their leader. "Someone has to stay with the sheriff, I can do that. No sense in all of us going to jail, you guys go ahead and get out of here."

The three of them shifted their feet, looking at each other. "Are you sure, boss?" Hardy asked.

Tucker clapped him on the back. "Sure, I'm sure. I'm thinking that maybe I'll retire. I'll do my time, then maybe find a job or something."

"A job! I swear, getting shot in the can musta addled your brains," Weaver said with great feeling.

Tucker laughed, waving the big outlaw off. "You guys get going. If them deputies come back, I'll stall them for a while."

Hardy and Danny brought the horses up, and prepared to leave. When Tucker started to help Marty on her horse, she balked. "If you are not going, then I'm staying with you," she said firmly.

"What about the gold?" Tucker asked.

"I don't care about that stuff anymore. Throw it in the lake for all I care," she said, spunkily. "All I want is to be with you."

Tucker caressed her cheek with his rough, brown hands. He looked in her eyes and saw she was serious. He dropped his hand and laughed nervously. "You want to go to the territorial prison?"

"No one said you were going to jail for sure," Marty replied. "They still have to have a trial and convict you. If they do, I'll wait."

A lump came into Tucker's throat, and he felt misty eyed. To cover his emotions, he turned to his men. "She's staying. Go ahead and take the gold. When you cash it in, deposit my share and Marty's with Wells Fargo in her name."

Weaver mounted his horse, and looked down at Tucker and Marty. "I hope you know what you are doing. I ain't exactly sure it's right, but I wish you all the luck."

Danny tipped his hat, mounted and followed Weaver. Hardy shook Marty's hand, then Tucker's. The outlaw seemed about to say something, then stopped. Without a word, he climbed aboard his horse. Gathering the lead rope, he led the pack horses away.

After they were gone, Tucker checked on the sheriff. The lawman's breathing was smooth and easy—a good sign in Tucker's mind. As Tucker looked at him, the sheriff's eyes fluttered open.

He looked curiously at Tucker. "I figured you'd be long gone by now," he said weakly.

"Naw, I wouldn't leave you. I like you too much for that," Tucker told him.

"Have my deputies come back yet?"

"Not yet. If they don't show up soon, I'll go looking for them," Tucker promised.

Beauford nodded, his eye lids drooping sleepily. "I'd appreciate it," he said, so low Tucker could barely hear him.

Tucker moved away to let the sheriff rest. Marty stepped up beside him, taking his arm. "Do you think the deputies will be back?" she asked.

"I don't know. I'm afraid they walked into a trap set by Mason. I think he lured them away to take a shot at getting the gold."

"Do you think he killed them?" Marty asked, horrified at the thought.

"I don't know, but I fear for the first two that left."

Marty pressed the derringer into Tucker's hand. "Keep this, when the deputies come back use it to escape. We could go to California. Nobody would know you there."

Tucker thought about it. "I've always wanted to raise horses. I heard California was good country for horses," he said, dreaming of the possibility. Then he shook his head. "I don't know if you want to spend your life looking over your shoulder. I can't ask you to do that."

"You don't have to ask, I'm volunteering," Marty said, with a hopeful smile. "Just think about it."

Minutes later, the four deputies rode in carrying a wounded man. When he saw who the injured man was, Tucker jumped up and rushed over to him.

"How is he?" Tucker asked, looking at Deke Carlin's weather-beaten face.

"Not so good," one of the deputies answered, his voice as cold as a mountain winter. The deputy drew his pistol and aimed it at Tucker. "What's going on here?" he asked looking at Sheriff Beauford.

Chapter Twenty-four

Tucker straightened slowly. All four deputies had their guns out and pointed right at him. Tucker spread his hands, trying to look peaceful as possible.

"He took a shot at the sheriff, and I killed him," Tucker said, pointing to Mason's body.

The deputy took the gun from Tucker's belt, then relaxed. "That's the feller that ambushed us," he said. The deputy looked embarrassed as he told the story. "We found two men lying on the trail. When we rode up to see what happened, one of them jumped up and pulled a gun on us. He tied us up and left."

"That's the way me and Bill found them," one of the other deputies said, digging his friend in the ribs.

"Hey, where did your men go?" the first deputy asked, noticing that Tucker's men were gone.

"They sorta wandered off. They'll be back soon, I reckon," Tucker said, with a shrug.

"Yeah, I bet," the deputy answered, a sarcastic twinge in his tone.

While Tucker talked with the men, Marty sat down beside Deke Carlin. "How are you feeling, Mister Carlin?" she asked.

"I've been better, but I reckon I'll live," Deke grunted.

"Do you still intend on killing Tucker?" Marty asked, giving Deke a direct, challenging stare.

Deke thought about it before he answered. "No. I don't

reckon I ever did mean to kill him. When I first said that, I was mad and talking out of turn. I never went looking for him. Fact is, I avoided finding him.''

"Tucker claimed that you blamed him for your parents death. Is that true?''

"I did at one time,'' Deke replied. "We had a farm in Missouri. Seemed like we was doing real good. Then the Masters clan moved in.''

"Who were they?''

"They were a rich family from the north. They moved into the area and sat up a bank. They made it real easy to borrow money, so our pa borrowed some to put in a bigger crop.''

"Anyway, just before harvest time our crop caught fire, and burned up. We weren't the only ones either, they was a rash of fires that summer.''

"The Masters set them?'' Marty asked.

"Sure they did. Well, come to find out, anyone that didn't pay their loan by the end of the summer lost their farm. With no crop to sell, we had no choice. We was packing to leave, when Tucker found out.''

Deke stopped to chuckle at the memory. "You should have seen him then. He was about fourteen, and ornery as a speckled pup. He was always into something. When Tucker learned we was losing the farm, he blew his top. He strapped on a gun and went to town. He had words with old man Masters. Upshot of the whole deal was Tucker killed Masters.''

Deke paused, growing tired, but wanting to finish the story. "Everyone who seen it claimed the old man went for his gun first and Tucker had to kill him. The law went after Tucker anyway, the marshal being a nephew of Masters. Tucker gave them the slip and hid out in the hills. When they lost Tucker, they came to our cabin, figuring Tucker would come home. When Tucker wasn't there, they up and killed our pa out of spite.''

''So that's how Tucker became an outlaw, by killing this man Masters?'' Marty asked, giving Deke a drink from a canteen.

''Well, that started it. The next night, Masters' bank was robbed. All the loan papers for everybody disappeared, along with a couple hundred dollars cash.''

Deke took another pull from the canteen and passed it to Sheriff Beauford. The lawman had been listening to Deke's story. Beauford took the canteen with a thoughtful expression on his face. The sheriff took a small drink and handed the canteen back to Marty.

''I stayed on the farm with Tucker's mother for a year, but then she passed away and I drifted. I think she just plain died from a broken heart.''

''What do you mean, Tucker's mother? I thought you two were brothers?'' Marty asked.

''Half brothers,'' Deke corrected. ''My own mother died in a smallpox epidemic. When I was about twelve, my father married Tucker's mother. Tucker came along a couple of years later.''

Deke leaned back, worn out from all his talking. ''You know, I spent all these years blaming Tucker for all that happened back there. I also blamed myself, I just didn't want to admit it.''

Deke closed his eyes, and balled his hands into fists. ''You see, I was gone when all this happened. Me and another guy took off on a wild goose chase to see the country. If I'd been home, working on the farm like I shoulda been, I might have stopped all of it.''

''I don't think either one of you was to blame,'' Marty said. ''But it's over now, you and Tucker should make up.''

"Did I hear my name?" Tucker asked, walking over to where they sat.

"We were talking about you," Marty told him. "Deke was telling me how you got started as an outlaw."

Tucker looked quickly to Deke. The older man returned Tucker's look with a steady stare of his own. Tucker tried to read his brother's thoughts, but could not.

For a second a tense silence hung over the small clearing. Marty cleared her throat, glancing from one brother to the other.

The sound of hoofbeats broke the tension, as all eyes swung to Pete and Delbert as they rode in.

"What happened here?" Pete asked, jumping off his horse.

"Never mind that. What are you doing back here?" Sheriff Beauford asked hoarsely.

Looking around to make sure everyone was listening, Pete told about his and Delbert's encounter. "I guess Tucker and his men were telling the truth after all," Pete concluded.

"Does that mean Tucker can go?" Marty asked quickly.

All eyes swung to Sheriff Beauford, who lay propped up on his saddle. The sheriff's face was drawn, and he had dark hollows under his eyes. "I guess he's cleared of our robbery, and the one in Del Norte. I suppose he can go."

Marty gave a little cheer and clapped her hands. Tucker cut her cerebration short. "I don't know if I want to go," he said.

Tucker turned to Marty. "What kind of life could we have? We'd be moving around all the time, always looking over our shoulders. You'd always have to worry about somebody getting off a lucky shot."

"I wouldn't care about that, as long as we were together," Marty said softly.

"It just wouldn't work. Somebody trying to build a reputation would always be after me,'' Tucker said, unable to keep the heartache he felt off his face.

"They wouldn't look for you. Not if you were dead,'' the deputy Pete put in.

"What do you mean?'' Tucker asked warily.

Pete pointed to where the other deputies were digging a grave for Mason. "Here lies the outlaw, Tucker Evans. Shot while trying to escape,'' he quoted. "I think it makes a fine epitaph.''

Tucker rubbed his jaw, thinking it over. Marty clenched her fists, waiting expectantly.

"We could tell a good story,'' Pete encouraged. "We arrested you, and recovered the money. While we were bringing you in, you got your hands on a gun and shot the sheriff.''

Pete paused, pointing his finger at Tucker like a gun. "Course I shot you while you were trying to escape.'' Pete looked to Delbert. "How 'bout it kid? Do you want to shoot him, too? It'd make you famous.''

Delbert thought about it. It would make him famous. "No,'' Delbert said finally. "I'm going to be a farmer and rancher. I don't need to be famous.''

"Suit yourself,'' Pete said with a shrug. He looked to where the other deputies had stopped their digging to listen. "How about you fellers? You want to be famous?''

They all wanted to be part of the story. While they hashed out the final details of the story, Tucker knelt beside Deke. He could hear the battle becoming larger by the minute.

"Sounds like a humdinger of a fight,'' Deke said. "That Tucker Evans sure was a hard man to kill, but I'm glad he's gone.'' Despite his wounded shoulder, Deke sat up and held out his hand. "I'd like to shake your hand, Tucker Carlin. It's good to see you again, little brother.''

Marty gave a squeal of delight, hugging both of them at

the same time. Tucker tilted his head back and gave her a kiss.

"Me and Marty was thinking of starting a horse ranch in California. We sure could use a partner," Tucker suggested.

"I'd like that," Deke said.

Tucker helped the posse finish burying Mason and put up the marker. They built a travois for the sheriff. When Tucker asked Deke if he needed one, Deke declined. "You just get me up on my horse and I'll be fine," Deke said gruffly.

Tucker pulled Delbert off to the side. "You going back to your dad's farm?"

"Yes, sir," Delbert replied. "That farm looks pretty good now."

"Before you head home, why don't you come to Santa Fe with us? We think you deserve a split of the gold," Tucker told him.

The shock Delbert felt showed on his smooth face. "But I helped Mason, when he tried to take the map from you," the youngster protested.

"We talked it over and it's all settled. We decided you earned a share," Marty encouraged, giving Delbert a friendly pat on the shoulder.

"I'd be glad to have the money. We could expand the farm, maybe buy some cattle," Delbert said, smiling gratefully.

"I thought you were going to take the money back to the bank," Pete said. "You'd be a hero."

"You take it to them. I don't want to be a hero," Delbert told him.

After the deputies loaded Sheriff Beauford on his travois, and set out at a very slow pace, Deke sat up. "Help me up on my horse, and we can be on the road."

"It'll be dark in a couple hours. We might as well stay here until morning," Tucker decided.

As darkness fell, Marty cooked over a fire, preparing the evening meal, when the cry came from the darkness.

"Hello, in the camp."

Tucker stood up, putting his hand to his gun. He smiled, sure that he recognized the voice. "Come on in," he called.

Weaver, Danny and Hardy rode in all smiles. "We hid back and watched the proceedings," Weaver told them. "You must have done some slick talking for them to let you go," he told Tucker.

"They didn't let me go," Tucker said, pointing to the grave.

Weaver bent closer, having trouble reading the marker in the dim light. "Well I'll be hanged," he said. "You're a corpse."

"We stuck around to make sure they didn't take you to jail," Danny said.

"I bet," Tucker shot back. "You stayed so Weaver could get one more meal."

"Is it ready?" Weaver asked, rubbing his hands together.

The next morning, they sat out for Santa Fe to cash in their treasure. "What are you boys going to do with your share," Tucker asked his men.

Weaver grinned broadly, looking very proud. "We talked it over last night. The two boys decided to go together and get themselves a place by Delbert's daddy's and go to ranching. I'm gonna go along to see that they do it right," the big outlaw said.

Tucker laughed at the thought. Them two youngsters would keep Weaver on his toes. "How about you Hardy?" Tucker asked.

Hardy smiled, showing his white teeth. "I think I'll just spend my share," he said.

"When we get to Santa Fe, we'll need to rest up a bit before I'm able to go to California," Deke said. "Be plenty of time for you two to get married."

Deke dug into his pocket and pulled out a gold ring. "This was the ring our pa gave to your mother. I thought maybe you'd like to give it to Marty," he said, handing the ring to Tucker.

Years later, when a brash young man named Tucker Evan Carlin was elected to the California State Congress, old Deke Carlin sat on his porch in his wheelchair. Old Deke shook his head. "Must be something about that name," he muttered. "But then there's a rotten apple in every barrel," he decided.